B–36 Cold War Shield

B-36 Cold War Shield

Navigator's Journal

by

Vito Lasala

authorHOUSE®

AuthorHouse™
1663 Liberty Drive
Bloomington, IN 47403
www.authorhouse.com
Phone: 1 (800) 839-8640

Published by AuthorHouse   06/02/2015

ISBN: 978-1-5049-1325-6 (sc)
ISBN: 978-1-5049-1358-4 (e)

Library of Congress Control Number: 2015908033

Print information available on the last page.

For
KAREN LASALA CARDELLA
who yearned to be an author

Grateful for technical assistance from
WILLIAM LASALA

Chapter One

Routine Fourteen-Hour

12 April 1954

Major Kingby, our aircraft commander, is in the lead as the three of us shuffle out of the 40th Bomb Squadron Operations Building into the predawn dark. The cool air feels good on my sweaty face.

We just completed a weather briefing inside, but Kingby still decides to tell us what we already know: "Weather briefing was short and simple. Looks as if we'll have few weather concerns today."

"Little turbulence and mostly blue sky above," I say. "My kind of day."

I'm First Lieutenant Hall, navigator, and to my right is our radar officer, Major Heller, who gives an approving grunt to my comment. Two Air Force blue stake-bed trucks sit thirty feet away, waiting for us, with engines off and headlights bright. As we walk toward the vehicles, the drivers see us, the truck engines rev up, and they move closer to meet us. Already on board the trucks are the rest of our crew, waiting for us. They are sitting on the flatbed of the vehicles, pressed up against a mound of crew bags, equipment, parachutes, and stacks of white boxes that hold our cold in-flight meals.

Major Kingby swings his map case and flight bag up onto the bed of the first truck, sings out "Good morning," and then walks up to the front of the truck and climbs into the cab. Heller and I hand our chart cases and flight bags up to the men already on the second vehicle, climb aboard, and sit on the truck bed with our legs comfortably hanging off the back end of the vehicle. Heller balls up a fist and slams it twice on the flatbed to signal to the driver that we're ready to go.

The vehicles lumber forward, grinding in low gear away from Operations and onto the aircraft parking apron. This feels familiar and comfortable, as we've done it dozens of times. Maybe with a different truck and driver, but with pretty much the same crew, many of whom are not quite fully awake. The field is quiet except for the noise of the trucks moving through the dark morning stillness. I can hear aircraft engines in the distance, winding up as a B-36 moves toward the runway. Sounds like one crew started its day even earlier than we did.

We're moving across the parking apron of Walker Air Force Base, located in about the center of the state of New Mexico. Walker is located in the middle of an endless flat and arid high desert, and thus the base is typically the target of dry winds that leave an ever-present layer of fine brown dust on every exposed surface. Walker is eight miles from the old, colorless town of Roswell, which clings to the air base for its very survival. Roswell is spoken of, with more than a little sarcasm, as the "Flower of the Desert." Beyond Roswell, Albuquerque is two hundred miles of unbroken desert to the northwest, and Santa Fe is located at the foot of the mountains about two hundred miles across desert to the northeast. To the south is Ciudad Juarez and El Paso, built on opposite sides of the Rio Grande River and both also about two hundred miles away across more of the same desert—with El Paso in Texas and Ciudad Juarez in Mexico.

I blink and bring myself out of my mental geographic wanderings. I take a deep breath through my nostrils, and the truck bed smells of old sweat, oil, gasoline, and diesel exhaust. After being in the vehicle even just a short while, I probably already smell the same.

Streaks of light, soft orange, now start to split the darkness to the east. The sun is just beginning to rise above the cool desert. Early sun rays, always orange, filter through the permanent layer of dust above the desert floor. *Would make a fine painting,* I consider, and then look to my right.

"Major," I say to Heller, "feels like you've done this before?"

"Too many times before," Heller growls. "I must be getting old."

I only nod and look back to the east. Major Heller *is* getting old, I think. He's probably forty-five by now. Heller flew in B-29's over the Pacific a long time ago.

At this time of the morning, Heller and I don't have much to say, but the young gunners in the vehicles are all now wide awake and raring to go, joking and chattering among themselves. I have been up for hours. My alarm jarred me awake at 0300, and after a quick shower, I walked through the dimly lit streets of the base to an almost empty Officers Club. Paul Panetta had just entered the Club, and we sat together for a quick breakfast of sausage, eggs, and coffee, and then walked back together to the BOQ—Bachelor Officer Quarters. Paul went to his room to pick up his gear and then waited in front of the building for one of the flatbed trucks to pick him up, but I gathered my flight bag and map case and loaded my gear into my car. I needed to be at the Flight Line Operations Building for that weather briefing at 0430 hours.

Now, sitting in the back of the truck, I imagined that all of the gunners rolled out of their bunks about an hour ago, taken a shower, and had breakfast at the enlisted mess. After loading their gear aboard the trucks, they probably sat waiting for the three of us, wondering why it always took so long for us to make ready for a flight. The gunners' hands-on preflight will start as soon as they board the aircraft, but until then, they have to wait … and wait.

"Hope nothing interferes with our shootout," says one of the gunners. "After cleaning, loading, and checking my guns under the sun all day yesterday, I want to hear my .50-caliber shells chatter and clunk!"

Tail Gunner Gordon snorts a laugh, then says, "Better get a hundred percent fire out or tomorrow you will back out in the sun again trying to explain to Captain Harris what went wrong."

Our full-crew flight briefing had been at 1400 hours yesterday. The flight is planned to be a routine fourteen-hour training mission around the flagpole, meaning that the flight would take off and land at Walker, not a destination field.

At the previous day's briefing, Major Kingby gave the flight requirements, altitudes in route, and some more information specific to the mission. As navigator, I outlined the flight plan route, and

3

the times and distances to meet the requirements set by Squadron Operations.

Major Heller, Radar Officer, closed the briefing with, "We have solid target information and photos. This mission will be with bomb bays empty. Weapon drop will be simulated and scored by a mobile scoring unit at the target site."

MAIN LANDING GEAR UNDER WING

Early this morning, I parked my car close to the Operations Building to cut down on the distance that I had to carry my map case and flight bag. Since my arctic jacket won't fit into my bulging flight bag, I always have to either wear it or carry it separately. This morning, I decided to wear it rather than carry it—and paid the price in sweat the entire time we were in the heated Ops Building for weather briefing.

On every flight, we are required to carry full arctic gear. It is always possible during a flight that, no matter what our mission outline, we could be diverted from our planned flight plan and destination. The Squadron and Wing staff always want to know how a crew handles unexpected changes while in flight. At some of our airfields in Alaska or Greenland, the outside temperature is so low that we have to wrap ourselves in arctic gear just to step out of the aircraft. Cabin heaters could malfunction at 25,000 feet, or we might receive orders to climb to 40,000 feet, where the arctic gear would be more than welcome.

My map case holds navigation charts for the mission, celestial tables, and plotting tools, plus any charts that we might need in case of a change en route called to us after takeoff.

In my flight bag, I always stow arctic boots, an insulated flight suit, gloves, a hat, toilet paper, one clean uniform, and anything else I think I might need before returning to Walker.

* * * * *

The sun now outlines the mountains beyond the dark desert. I can hear the change in pitch of the engines of that B-36 with an early scheduled takeoff as the aircraft maneuvers toward the runway. Our trucks approach the long line of parked B-36 aircraft, and the dark silhouette of each plane looms larger as we draw close. Our truck headlights reflect brightly off the aluminum skin until we flash by and look to the next aircraft in line. The trucks make a smooth stop at our assigned B-36, keeping a respectable distance from the aircraft. I slide off the stake-bed, lift my flight bag onto my shoulder, and grab my map case. The trucks remain idling as the crew unloads all the gear.

"Have a good flight," calls one of the truck drivers as both men turn their vehicles and drive back toward the Operations Building.

Kingby lifts his arm in acknowledgment, grabs his gear, and turns to the job at hand.

DARK SILHOUETTE.........HEADLIGHTS REFLECT

I imagine the drivers would rather be part of our crew, getting ready to fly instead of driving a vehicle back to the Ops Building.

I again hear the change in pitch of the engines of that B-36 across the field. It must be at the end of the runway. The whining cry of the jet engines coming online joins in, and the engine noise grows louder as the pilot brings all ten engines to full power. Should be rolling now.

Following Kingby, Major Heller and I start moving toward the nose wheel of our aircraft. The increasing engine noise in the distance fills the quiet morning as the plane starts its takeoff roll. Routine.

Suddenly, everyone stops moving. Heads snap up to listen. No engine noise! Deadly quiet.

Abort! That B-36 has cut all engines. Aborted takeoff!

We all stand motionless and listen. Across the airfield, a puff of yellow smoke rises from the direction of the runways.

"Shit," someone groans. "She's down and hurting."

Truck sirens wail. From a low, one-story building located close to the far side of the runway, we can hear the sound of fire trucks as they race toward the smoke, quickly followed by the sound of heavier vehicles that are probably fitted with cranes and special equipment.

Then, from behind us, emergency-alert horns blare to life all over the base, drowning out everything else. I look toward the base and I can see flashing red lights on white vehicles from the base hospital moving as fast as they can go. They speed through the now wide-open gates in the chain-link fence located between the flight line and the base, making loud whupping noises that clear the way. Close behind the ambulances stream a cluster of jeeps and a small truck, all full of hospital staff.

Thirty seconds behind them, trucks from base fire protection race through the gates. They are painted a bright yellow, sounding their sirens that demand "Get the hell out of the way!" The dreaded yellow trucks always stir up fear and anxiety. On our field, yellow trucks always mean trouble.

When the base emergency horns squall, every first responder runs full-out to his station and follows the orders that have just arrived at his station seconds earlier. Losing seconds may mean losing lives.

The air is electric. Near our aircraft, we are all still standing in the spots we were when the noise of the aircraft engines suddenly stopped.

"Move it!" Major Kingby finally bellows. "Standing there with your mouths hanging open does no one any good. Do your job."

Everyone jerks back to the here and now, grabs something, and moves toward our B-36 again. Muttered conversations do not slow the activity.

I hear, "Son of a bitch. What a way to start the day. Whose plane is it? Not 40th, I hope."

No one dares to slow down, but heads keep popping up, with eyes turning toward the smoke. I set my bags on the apron as the crew forms two lines in front of the nose wheel assembly.

* * * * *

A B-36 standard crew numbers fifteen men. Stationed in the forward pressurized cabin are the aircraft commander, second pilot, third pilot, engineer, second engineer, radar officer, navigator, observer, radio operator, and second radio. The aft pressurized cabin has five stations, manned by four gunners located two on each side of the compartment, and a tail gunner. All five gunners rotate into the scanner positions, which are located at small, clear plastic bubbles, one at each side of the rear cabin. From those ports, the scanners can see forward and are charged with monitoring the engines on their side of the aircraft. Highest-ranking enlisted man runs the show in the aft cabin.

For our forward crew this trip, the second engineer and second radio slots are unfilled, so presently we are a crew totaling thirteen.

* * * * *

Major Kingby stands out front, facing the crew. "At the runway, first responders are doing their jobs, people who are better trained to help than we are and have the tools and equipment they need."

Kingby is career Air Force and he looks it. His flight suit is spotless, ironed, and even has a crease at the legs. No small accomplishment. We all know, including the major, that the creases will be gone ten minutes after boarding our aircraft. Makes no difference.

For early morning flights, Major Kingby is always clean shaven and clear eyed. When we have a night takeoff, Kingby's face looks unshaven by 1700 hours as his black stubble grows in. This annoys the hell out of him, since he is always very particular about his appearance when in uniform. Rarely does he smile. He has a serious job and his responsibilities weigh heavily on him.

Flight suits, worn by all crewmen, are gray, one-piece, long-sleeved jumpsuits with a heavy-duty zipper that runs from collar to crotch. Flight suits need to be oversized and droopy to allow for freedom of movement. One zippered pocket is sewn on the upper-left sleeve, next to the slots for pens and pencils. Two pockets are located at the chest, two at the thighs, and one more at the outer side of each lower leg, all with zippers. When the pockets are stuffed with all that we need or think we might need close at hand, the suits bulge and sag and look like hell.

Of course, after preflight preparation, a fourteen-hour flight, and post-flight debriefing, our aircraft commander looks like the rest of us: tired, sweat soaked, and red eyed, with stubbly hair on his face.

Major Kingby begins his standard pre-boarding instructions: "This is a fourteen-hour training mission. We are carrying no weapon in the bomb bay, but navigation legs, gunner's shootout, radio procedures, optimum fuel consumption, and accuracy of simulated weapon drop will all be scored. Fly safe, stay alert, and maintain intercom discipline. All runways are clear and usable. Let's get on board."

Carrying his flight bag and map case, Kingby heads for the ladder to the forward compartment. The second pilot, Captain Harris, and the first engineer, Captain Cruz, leave their gear on the apron and start their walk-around aircraft inspection. The rest of the forward cabin crew follow Kingby up the ladder, each man carrying his gear, and they begin their individual preflight checklists.

Gunners carry their flight bags to the aft cabin ladder, load in, and then begin their own check of turrets, guns, and remote firing systems.

I push my flight bag ahead of me and struggle up the ladder. Master Sergeant Snell, our first radio, is already on board. With a mournful "Good Morning," he pulls my bag up, then my map case.

"Thanks, and a good morning to you, Sergeant," I reply. "Let's hope for an uneventful ride."

I take a couple of paces forward through the radio room and then bend over so I can stomp down the three steps into the forward lower-deck radar room. My flight bag stays in the radio room against the rear bulkhead, because the radar compartment has no room for it. I reach back for my map case and move forward to my station. The navigator's chair is bolted to the deck. I slide onto the leather seat, and swing to face my work table and instruments, which are mounted on the left side wall of the radar compartment. I begin to run through my preflight checklist.

Panetta is right behind me, and I ask him, "Have you checked the sextant and mount?"

Lieutenant Panetta, our observer, assists radar and navigator, and fills in at either position when needed during flight.

"Sextant checks out okay and is stowed," Panetta replies. "I'm reviewing target information with Radar. Will complete in about five minutes."

Standing up, I strap on my parachute harness. I reach down with my left hand and feel for the security of my chest pack on the floor, three inches from my left boot. During any flight, I may move within the aircraft to take a celestial shot from the dome, talk to Radio, or to take a piss, but I always know where that chute is and never stray too far from it.

Sometimes I wonder if I could really open the side hatch of the forward compartment and roll out into 25,000 feet of nothing but air. *Hope I never have to put that to a test.* Many guys have done it before out of all kinds of aircraft. *Would shit in my pants for sure.*

I turned on the long-range navigation—LORAN—set when I first sat down at my station, and now I calibrate the receiver. LORAN is not useful over the continental USA and is unreliable over water. The LORAN system is a navigational aid used by aircraft and ships at sea. Radio transmission towers are located on the coastline at the perimeter of the North Pacific Ocean. The tower signals can be picked up by our LORAN receivers on aircraft to give directional information to assist in navigation. It is an old system and can be disrupted by bad weather and other signals in the air. It is worthless, but my preflight demands that I make it ready and I do so. I make it ready because when we train, we train like it's the real thing. I'm ready to taxi.

The entire right side wall of the lower deck of the forward space is taken up by a radar scope and console, bomb monitoring instruments, radar flight panels, and numerous black boxes. Major Heller sits facing this overwhelming array of dials, screens, and controls. His duty as radar/bomber is to identify our target, and actually take over flight control of the aircraft from the pilots as we pass the Initial Point on a bomb run. Using his radar, he would fly the B-36 as we close on target and then release the weapon. He has prime responsibility for the weapon as soon as it's loaded into the bomb bay until release over target.

The entire forward wall of the compartment is an aluminum-ribbed clear Plexiglas bubble, eight feet in the diameter, extending floor to ceiling and wall to wall. When I sit in my chair at my station, my right foot rests on the aluminum frame around the bubble. We call it the "greenhouse." When I lean into the greenhouse, I can see activity on the paving directly below the aircraft. The greenhouse is big enough to stand in, if you don't mind standing on clear plastic, looking down between your boots at the terrain 25,000 feet below. Our radar room is an "office" in the sky. Right now, morning light streams into our office.

The aircraft commander activates the intercom: "This is the pilot for preflight status. Copilot?"

"Copilot, preflight complete. Tower clears us for taxi."

"Engineer?"

"Engineer, preflight complete. Ready for engine start."

"Radar?"

"Radar, preflight complete."

"Navigator?"

"Navigator, preflight complete."

"Radio?"

"Radio, preflight complete. Frequencies set in."

"Chief Gunner?"

"Chief Gunner. Aft compartment preflight complete. Scanners at stations."

Second Pilot clears with ground personnel and then checks in with the tower. We are cleared to start engines.

One by one, all six reciprocating engines crank, sputter, and rumble to life. The vibration jars every nerve ending. The noise and vibration will be with us until engine shutdown at the end of the mission.

Engines power up and the mighty B-36 moves slowly forward, then turns onto a taxiway. We roll to the end of the taxiway, turn, and line up on the runway.

"Assume takeoff positions," the flight deck orders.

All crew members in the forward compartment grumble, curse, crowd into the radio room, and sit on the floor with our backs against the front bulkhead of the radio room. On takeoff, most of us would rather remain at crew positions where we can see what is happening, instead of being stuffed into the radio room.

I believe that the survival rate from a crash on takeoff of a fuel-loaded B-36 is nil, whether you are at your station or on the floor of the radio room. None of us in the radio room are on intercom except Sergeant Snell. He is sitting on the floor but has rigged up an extension cord so he can still listen in on the intercom. The rest of us sit and wait and listen.

The engines, located on the trailing edge of the wings, are so far aft of the flight deck that neither the pilots nor the engineer can see them. Scanners in the aft cabin are stationed at Plexiglas bubbles, which are also gunner's positions on each side of the aircraft, giving them the all-important duty of being the eyes of the pilots and engineer. From a bubble, each scanner can see all three pusher and the two jet engines on his side of the aircraft. His job is to constantly watch the engines during the entire flight, searching for any abnormalities or malfunctions, no matter how minor. Scanners need to be especially vigilant during takeoff and landings, and their stations have direct communication with the flight deck. Crew in the aft cabin rotate into the scanner positions for the entire flight, so that the positions are always manned and the scanners remain wide awake, clear eyed, and alert.

After engines are run up, checklists are completed, and the pilots have clearance from the tower, engines are brought up to full power. I feel a small lunge as we start our takeoff roll. The ponderous, magnificent B-36, with all engines thundering and the four jets whining, slowly moves forward, rolling into a laborious but steady takeoff.

The roll before liftoff always seems twice as long as it should, and I silently urge the B-36, "Up, dammit, up."

I feel the lifting off of the runway, the nose assembly off first and ten seconds later the main gears following. I check my watch so I can record the takeoff time. As the plane strains for altitude, I leave the radio room and have an uphill climb to reach my seat up front in the radar room. I start my log: *Takeoff at 0622 hours.*

At the weather briefing this morning, we received information about estimated winds and cloud coverage. I determine the initial heading using the preflight wind information, which is the best I have available at the time.

"Navigator to Pilot."

"Pilot, go ahead Navigator."

"Navigator. Initial heading to Lubbock, zero eight four degrees."

"Pilot, confirm heading zero eight four."

The aircraft dips a wing, and turbulence from ground updrafts batters us as we continue to climb. I know that the rough bouncing won't last long and I hang on. I check out the LORAN and, as my reward, get clutter and static, and then I turn the damn thing off.

The basic method of navigating in flight is called "dead reckoning," as it is for ships at sea, aided by celestial, directional radio signals and radar. On training missions, directional radio signals received by the pilots and radar information are, by design, not made available to the navigator. We train without making use of those navigational aids because, at times, radar breaks down, and at times of national emergency, directional radio transmitters are shut down.

The mission profile from Squadron Ops dictates the training schedule that must be met on each leg of the flight. Each crew member has his own training segment to compete, and right now, all are running an in-flight check of all their equipment.

Major Heller shouts over the engine roar, "Radar is up and running and checks out."

I lift my hand to acknowledge.

The engine noise is so loud and continuous that, in the radar compartment, we have to yell to each other to be heard. It takes a lot of effort to shout all the time, and it is tiring after a while, but we need to stay off intercom as much as possible. Normally, we use hand signals to communicate in the radar room if we are able to catch the eye of our fellow crew member.

* * * * *

The traditional method of creating a bomber flight crew over the years had been to assemble a group of men into a tight, well-knit team who trained together and always flew as a unit. Today, a less romantic concept applies.

Men who fly in General LeMay's Strategic Air Command are part of a combat war machine. Each member of every crew is trained to a standard of performance set for his position in the aircraft. When he is belted into his designated position of the aircraft, he becomes part of that machine. Each crewman is expected to be able to board a B-36 aircraft that he has never flown in before, become part of a crew he has never seen before, know what is expected of him, and do his job. Every crew member is an interchangeable part of that flying machine. The machine, made up of men and material, is designed for only one task: to deliver a nuclear weapon on a designated target.

* * * * *

The crew settle into their stations. The intercom is silent. Our AC— air commander—is real tight about intercom discipline.

"Stay off the internet," Kingby tells us, "unless you have something worth talking about."

Our heading is east, and the glare of that golden rising sun is intense through the greenhouse. Bright and blinding. My only protection is my sunglasses, my baseball-type cap that I pull down low over my face, and a piece of cardboard that I have temporarily taped up so that it hangs vertically at my table, keeping part of my chart in shadow.

"You getting a suntan?" I ask Heller.

He has his face jammed into the radar eye shield and his flight cap tilted low against the sun. All he does is wave his arm in acknowledgement. I usually have little to say; Heller usually has less.

The aircraft climbs through a thin broken layer of clouds at 15,000 feet and continues to climb into a clear blue sky. This flight is scheduled to be flown at 25,000 feet, so cabin pressure will be at about 9000 feet and we won't need our oxygen masks. I keep my mask close by anyway. Explosive decompression is always a possibility, and if that ever happens, our cabin pressure would immediately slam up to 25,000 feet and we would be scrambling for our masks in a cabin full of fog. The mask and air tube are cumbersome, uncomfortable, and always seem to be in the way, so we use them only when absolutely necessary.

* * * * *

The B-36 is a big bird. It is 163 feet long with a wingspan of 230 feet, and today our bird is manned by a crew of thirteen. When the crew is augmented by the luxury of a second radio operator and a second engineer, then we become a standard B-36 crew of fifteen. Three pusher engines are mounted on the trailing edge of each wing. This aircraft that we've been assigned is a Model D, on which have been added two jet pods outboard of the three reciprocating engines on each wing. The Model D, with an unbelievable total of ten engines, gives this B-36 a combat range of 4,200 miles. This aircraft, flying at 435 miles per hour and at 40,000-foot altitude, can deliver a 10,000-pound nuclear weapon on its designated target and return to its forward base of departure.

The flight deck is located directly above our radar deck, and although their windscreens are tinted, I'm sure the pilots are squinting through sunglasses and will be acquiring quality suntans as we fly into the sun. Together with the radio room, located just aft of the two decks, these three spaces make up our forward compartment. The bomb bays extend from immediately behind the rear wall of the radio room, to the forward bulkhead of the rear pressurized compartment.

Access to the flight deck is from the front of the radio room, by way of climbing up a few metal steps. The pilots sit side by side under a tinted Plexiglas dome, which gives them good visibility forward, above, and on each side. Their visibility aft, though: none. This gigantic flying machine is all aft of the flight deck, out of sight of the pilots and engineer. The pilots' seats are surrounded by flight and engine controls, dials, instruments, gauges, and radios. Instrument panels are located above and below the windscreens, directly overhead, and on both sides of the space. To get to their seats, the pilots need to bend at the waist, slide between the two seats, and finally fall forward and to the left or right into their position.

Behind the pilots' seats, the engineer sits at a small table facing the right sidewall of the flight deck. He monitors an array of instruments, gauges, and indicators. He tracks all systems for the six reciprocal engines and four jet engines, and is confronted by what looks like an overwhelming number of instruments monitoring all systems and backup systems in the plane: hydraulic, electrical, oxygen, fuel, oil, heating, cabin pressure, and fire suppression. The engineer maintains a flight log and is responsible for fuel management to provide for maximum efficiency in flight. Every usable space on the flight deck is crammed with the ever-present black boxes. The engineer is constantly scanning his panels, looking for any abnormalities or problems.

The pilots and engineer keep their seat belts buckled loosely at all times. No one, but no one, climbs the steps to the flight deck without an invitation. The small platform used by the observer or navigator to stand on while taking celestial observations is located most of the way up those same steps. The platform is to one side of the steps and just big enough to hold two flight boots. It is as far up the steps as we go unless we have a damn good reason to go farther. We are ignored and looked upon as intruders by the crew on the flight deck.

* * * * *

The roar of the engines decreases as we level out at 25,000 feet. The pilots ease back on our six reciprocal engines, and the jet engines are idled and taken offline. I signal Panetta to come close,

"Take a sun shot as soon as the plane settles and holds steady," I say. "Let's make sure our watches are still reading the same."

We compare our watches and Panetta nods.

"I'm on my way," he says.

He pulls the sextant from its box, turns, and makes his way up the few steps toward the flight deck. Standing on the small platform, he hangs the sextant onto its hook in the celestial dome, records the time, and then "shoots the sun." He sights on the sun through the sextant, keeping the bubble centered and holding steady against the movement of the aircraft. Then he records his times and readings, and comes back down and hands me the information. I use the shoot times, sextant readings, and the sun navigation tables to plot the fix on my chart. It shows our location only four miles south of our planned track, so we maintain the same heading.

I sit back away from my nav table and take a few deep breaths. Panetta is working with Heller now, peering into the radar scope over his shoulder, and I look out the greenhouse and enjoy the thin layer of clouds below and the clear blue sky above. No turbulence. A solid, steady drone of the engines and we are heading into the bright yellow sun rising directly in front of us.

At 25,000 feet, the ground is visible through broken clouds, so I can map-read, constantly comparing ground features with my chart.

Fifty minutes after our first sun shot, Panetta takes another. I plot the fix nine miles off of our planned course, calculate the wind and call the pilot with a small change of heading. Panetta sits on a blanket on the cold edge of the greenhouse frame and map-reads. We take turns using the sextant once every hour and plotting the fixes. Map-reading and occasional sun shots work out well for quite a while.

THE B-36 IS A BIG BIRD

On my way to the celestial dome, I ask Radio, "Anything new from the flight deck?"

Sergeant Snell knows that what I'm asking about is the condition of the plane, since he is in the loop when the pilot reports to Walker on aircraft status.

"Number five has been losing oil and the flight deck has shut it down," Snell says. "Nothing on the radio about the B-36 abort back at Walker."

I signal "Thank you" with a silent nod. Crew members not on the flight deck are not kept aware of the status of the aircraft unless an emergency arises and the aircraft commander notifies the crew, but Sergeant Snell brings me up to date whenever I ask him.

There won't be any chatter about the aborted takeoff on any military radio, I know. Information about incidents involving B-36 aircraft is immediately classified as *SECRET* by Strategic Air Command. We never see a newspaper article or hear a news item on radio or TV about any SAC units. By the time we land back at Walker, anyone on base will be able to tell us all the details about the plane and crew because word on base spreads quickly. No official information of any kind leaves the base, though. Walker absorbs the loss, the pain and the sorrow. Families and friends will grieve. Base hospital will do its best to mend the broken bodies and minds.

The old-timers have told us that our current tradition began in the past: when there is a loss of life in the air, there is a quiet church memorial service. The memorial service is always well attended and people who cannot get into the overflowing base church stand outside through the entire service. Traditionally, the dead crew members are cremated and buried together. An aircraft is then brought up out of the reserve group of planes and takes its place in the active line on the apron. Crew members are reassigned, and men recently graduated from the various schools are mixed in with experienced crew members. Another flying machine, made up of aircraft and men, takes the place of the lost B-36. Two weeks later, the grief and pain will still remain, for a long time, but on the base and flight line, all the routines return. Normal.

We'll hear the news when we return to Walker.

* * * * *

At fifty miles west of Lubbock, we are still drifting a little south of our planned course.

"Navigator to Pilot."

"Pilot here."

"New heading to Norman, Oklahoma, zero seven two degrees.

"Pilot to Navigator, understand new heading now, zero seven two degrees."

As the pilot makes the turn, Lubbock appears off our left wing, and we bypass it on our way to Norman. Lubbock is an easy map-read. It sits all by itself in a vast area of open Texas country.

I remember reading about Lubbock a few years ago. Must have been in 1951 when the city had its day of national recognition. Seems that a V-shaped formation of lights flew over the city, observed by everyone, including many scientists at local universities. Called the "Lubbock Lights," many theories were offered about what they were and where they came from. One popular theory bandied about was that newly installed city street lights reflected off a flock of birds, giving the appearance of lights. To this day, the Lubbock Lights have never been fully explained, and their source is still determined as *Unknown*.

The leg from Lubbock to Norman is less than two hours long.

As we close on Norman, we hear over the intercom: "Crew, this is the Flight Deck. Latest weather shows an unexpected severe weather system blowing in from the Gulf over New Orleans and heading north. The weather system is expected to bring with it heavy rain, strong winds aloft, and very active electrical disturbances. The system may cause us to make a change in our flight plan. We will keep you informed."

A careful look out of the greenhouse gives no hint of a change in local weather. Broken cloud cover below and very few clouds above. Radar will pick up the expected increase in cloud cover long before we see it, but radar can't see any wind shift or increase of velocity. Weather looks great right now, but the area surrounding Oklahoma City, including Norman, is known as "Tornado Alley." From March through June each year, the land is subjected to more tornados than any other region within the United States. Lots of damage every year. We need to steer clear of any weather system in this part of the country.

Ten minutes after our change in heading over Norman, we hear: "This is Major Kingby. Weather from the Gulf is moving north rapidly. We have a choice of flying on top or going around, and I have elected to go around. Tops of cumulus clouds at 33,000 feet and still building."

A few minutes later: "Major Kingby here. We shall continue with original flight plan to Fort Smith, Texas. Weather Service recommends we stay north of Memphis, Tennessee. Navigator, plot a new course out of Fort Smith, staying north of Memphis, to our target city of Raleigh. Notify me when you complete."

"Navigator to Pilot, understand."

Twenty minutes later: "Navigator to Pilot."

"Pilot."

"Navigator, have new course plotted. I can pass chart up or bring it to you for review."

"I'm on my way down."

Major Kingby appears on the lower deck. I get out of my seat so he can sit in it and look at my chart.

He scans the chart for a minute, then says, "Walk me through it."

"Out of Fort Smith, we head north of east to Nashville instead of southeast to Greenwood. That will carry us about seventy-five miles north of Memphis." I place my finger on Memphis. "From Nashville, we would turn almost directly east, passing over Knoxville, Tennessee, then continue east to Raleigh. We would be at Raleigh about twenty minutes sooner than our original plan."

Kingby looks at the chart two minutes longer. "I'll lose the twenty minutes with airspeed. Looks good to me," he says as he rises. "Let's do it."

We fly the new route, carrying us north of Memphis, and at 0952 hours turn onto a long leg to Nashville, a little over 500 miles.

I call out to Panetta, "Paul, how about sitting in for a while?"

"I'm ready," he responds.

"Cloud coverage increasing below. Looks like 25 percent now. Map-reading still good but cross-check with sun shots," I relay to him.

"No problem."

"Give me half an hour."

I move back into the radio compartment. I piss into the tube, drink a full bottle of water, chew on a chocolate bar, and then lie on the flight bags piled on the floor in the corner of the radio room. I close my eyes and listen to the engine drone, and I can feel the vibrations through the floor.

Seems like one minute later, I feel Sergeant Snell nudging me with his boot until I wake up.

"Lieutenant Panetta says your half-hour is gone."

"Thanks," I mumble.

Panetta slides out so I can drop into the nav seat. He cheerfully tells me he just completed a sun shot. It plotted well and we will be passing north of Little Rock in a few minutes.

"Thanks," I mumble yet again.

I gulp half a bottle of water and look over the chart. After a short time, through the greenhouse, I can just see Little Rock in the distance off our right wing, jutting above the ground haze. Map-reading here is a piece of cake. I can see the sun reflecting off the fat, lazy Mississippi River a short time later, with Route 55 paralleling just west of the river. We cross the river twenty miles north of course and maintain our heading. I plot a map-reading fix as we cross over the river.

Thirty minutes later, I shoot the sun and plot. Twenty minutes before reaching Nashville, I call: "Pilot, Navigator."

"Pilot."

"Navigator. New heading now zero nine six degrees to Knoxville. We will be passing twenty miles north of Nashville."

"Pilot to Navigator, understand new heading, zero nine six degrees."

* * * * *

All crew members are required to complete and log their training requirements on each leg. Gunners must, at altitude, check out sighting and remote tracking systems, and fire all ammo, recording any reason they do not have 100 percent fire-out. Radar tracks our course and the pilots monitor our flight using directional radio beacons. Radio is in contact with ground facilities along our entire route.

About one hour later, we fly over the well-known town of Oak Ridge, Tennessee, just a few miles west of Knoxville. Over Knoxville, a small change in heading puts us on the path to Raleigh, which will be a ninety-minute leg.

The entire crew is now wide awake. The purpose of this mission is to make a practice bomb run over a precise target in Raleigh, and we are getting close. Panetta is working with Heller, reviewing and checking the location of the Initial Point and the target information.

The tension runs deep, but everyone looks calm. Just do the job.

"Navigator to Pilot."

"Pilot here."

"Navigator. Heading is zero nine four degrees to the Initial Point. ETA to IP is 1332 hours."

"Pilot to Navigator, heading to IP is zero nine four degrees."

I sit back, place my hands on my table, and look out the greenhouse dome. We're coming up on Raleigh.

Our bomb run over Raleigh will be at 25,000 feet. In a combat situation, we would carry the weight of a weapon up to 40,000 feet and release from that altitude.

The Initial Point—IP—has been selected by Radar, and I have provided a heading and estimated time to his IP. As we close on the IP, the pilot brings all jets online. The pilot makes his turn over the IP and brings all reciprocating engines and jets to full power for the bomb run. The increase in vibration makes my whole body shake. The engine noise is a thundering, mind-numbing roar.

"Pilot to Radar."

"This is Radar."

"Radar, we have completed our turn over the IP and are on a heading to target."

The pilots take their hands and feet off the controls. Sweating now, they don't know what to do with their hands and feet. Their eyes keep searching the sky and their instrument panels for any problems. The pilots have given up control of the aircraft. We leave the IP and …

"Radar to Pilot, commencing bomb run."

"Pilot to Radar, you have control of the aircraft."

Radar acknowledges, "I have control."

Radar locates his precise target in Raleigh, and checks his target photos. Heller sets his radar marker on target, and the radar system automatically turns and holds the B-36 on a heading to the target.

Panetta is at Heller's shoulder checking and confirming every move taken by Radar. Major Heller maintains target set, and the aircraft continues to adjust heading to remain on target. The engines howl.

"Radar to Pilot, thirty seconds."

"Pilot, thirty seconds."

All other crew members scan the skies and remain silent. The vibration is overpowering.

Seems like a hell of a lot longer than thirty seconds.

Radar calls, "Bomb release!"

Pilot responds, "I have control," and grabs the control column.

If we had released a full-weight dummy or combat weapon, the crew would already have known when release had occurred. Dropping a MK-6 weapon weighing 8,500 pounds would cause the B-36 to leap vertically from the loss of weight, especially at 40,000 feet.

I have my seat belt tightened, have cleared my table, and I'm gripping the aircraft frame in anticipation of the next movement. I know what's coming next. Hearing "Bomb release," the pilot, with all ten engines still at full power, makes a very steep, climbing 180-degree turn away from the target. The vibration is gut wrenching. We all know that the B-36 was never designed to make a maneuver like this. The engines strain and moan until we level off, and then we are running from the target as fast as we can with all engines still at full power.

The motivation for this radical and dangerous maneuver is self-preservation. On a combat mission, the release of our nuclear weapon demands that we be as far away as possible from the blast to increase our chance of surviving. The blast's shock, heat, radiation, and debris would envelop our aircraft, and the greater distance from the target, the less chance of damage or destruction to our plane and to us. No one knows if a B-36 can escape unharmed after dropping a nuclear weapon from 40,000 feet. The Air Force has results of ground tests and projections, but no one actually knows. Well, maybe the big brass knows, but ...

Vehicles with scoring equipment were placed on land closest to the drop area earlier in the day, and the aircraft commander and radar officer will learn the accuracy of our bomb drop when we return to Walker.

We have only simulated a nuclear drop, but the escape maneuver is real enough, although at 25,000 feet instead of 40,000 feet. Sweat covers my face and nausea pulls at my gut as I watch the turn through the greenhouse. I am physically drained. I lower my head onto my arms on the tabletop and take deep breaths for a sixty-second count.

I have sat through that turn enough times now, but it doesn't get any easier.

"Navigator to Pilot."

"Pilot."

"New heading," I call. "Two five two to Bessemer, Alabama.

"Pilot, acknowledge two five two, Bessemer."

My nausea lessens after a while, and I bring the log up to date. I take a quick sun shot, plot the fix, and give up the station to Panetta. He is still discussing the bomb run and target review with Radar, but interrupts, plugs in his headset, and takes the navigator chair.

The pilot shuts down the jets and gradually reduces power to normal cruise. I retreat to the radio room, use the relief tube, and sit on the steps. From my boxed flight lunch, I eat a candy bar, chew on a chicken leg, finish up with chocolate pudding, and then drain a bottle of water.

"Panetta, give me twenty minutes," I yell.

Panetta gives me a thumbs-up. "Twenty minutes,"

I move away from the steps to the radio room to get out of the way, lie on the floor, close my eyes, and listen to the deep rumble of engines. My body tunes in to the engine vibrations through the floor.

Immediately, it seems, Snell is again gently kicking my leg with his boot until I lift my head. "Lieutenant Panetta says your twenty minutes are gone."

I continue to lie on the floor for another thirty seconds, wishing that I didn't have to move.

I don't remember falling asleep.

While I slept, Panetta took another celestial reading, plotted the fix, and called the pilot with a heading change to Bessemer. I sit in and Panetta turns back to work with Radar.

We change heading over Bessemer and continue on to Baton Rouge, Louisiana, then on to Waco, Texas. Over Waco, I call a new heading to the flight deck and continue to map-read and shoot the sun to find our way back to Walker.

At dusk, the sun drops too low in the sky to use as a celestial target any longer. The stars show early at altitude, and after a while, I am able to shoot the stars as celestial targets. We are two hours out of Walker.

I step back to Sergeant Snell's station and ask, "Anything new from upstairs?"

"Number five still shut down and number three running hot, but still online."

"Thanks."

The aircraft is close to planned flight course, and the mission requirements are complete. We are not on the ground yet, but everyone is easing up, except for the pilots. For them, the most demanding maneuver of the flight is still ahead: a night landing.

Major Heller is asleep at his station. He resists giving up his radar to Panetta or anyone else. Heller finally stirs and breaks into his flight lunch while completing his log and forms. Panetta, meanwhile, is sitting in the radio room on his flight bag with his eyes closed. I can't tell if he's asleep or not and I don't know how much he has slept in the last fourteen hours.

The last leg of our flight is over empty high desert. Through the greenhouse, all is dark below except for the lights from a few small towns as we fly over. Pilots have made a gradual descent so as to be at landing pattern altitude as we near Walker.

"Pilot to crew, prepare for landing," says a tired voice from the flight deck.

With all loose items stowed or secured, Heller, Panetta, and I move to the radio compartment and sit on the floor again, with our backs against the forward bulkhead. The third pilot comes down from the flight deck and joins us, sitting with his back against the bulkhead. I close my eyes, listen to the engine noise change, and feel the turns as the pilot flies the landing pattern.

A long whining noise followed by a loud clunk tells me that the main landing gear is locked down, and soon after, a light thud comes from the nose wheel assembly.

Thump! Thud!

We are on the runway and rolling. Brakes squeal, pressing us against the bulkhead. I don't think anyone ever sleeps through a landing. We return to our stations as the aircraft turns onto the taxiway and apron, and slowly moves to our spot in the long line of B-36's. Through the small window in our emergency exit door in the radio room, I can see the left-side wing walker holding a bright white light, assuring clearances as we taxi.

Full stop.

The engines are shut down, and the lack of engine noise and vibration is unsettling. The engineer completes his log, and the hatches are opened. No noise. No vibration. Different, like I've forgotten something but don't know what it is.

I don't feel the need to say anything. Guess I could say, "Made it again!" but I'm too tired to try to make a stupid joke.

The engineer and pilots stomp down from the flight deck, passing down map cases, equipment, and flight lunch trash. They then climb down the hatch ladder slowly and carefully all looking weary and red eyed. Everyone picks up his gear as he reaches the asphalt.

The rest of us follow, and I can see the crew from the aft cabin moving forward loaded down with their own flight bags. I smell like stale sweat. Two stake-bed trucks, painted the familiar and comfortable Air Force blue, stand by, with their tailgates open toward us, motors off, quiet and dark.

As Major Kingby approaches, the truck engines come to life and the drivers turn on their headlights. Ground maintenance crews are already standing by at their vehicles, parked near the nose of our B-36, ready to start their chores. The truck driver is standing on the flatbed of his truck before Major Kingby reaches the vehicle. The driver grabs the bags Kingby offers up and stows them aside so that they are off-loaded first. The rest of us board the vehicles, handing our bags to those already on board. Major Kingby has been walking around near the front of the trucks to loosen up from the stress of getting the big bird safely on the ground, but when we are all loaded up, he climbs into the passenger seat and we head for the welcoming glow of the well-lit Flight Ops Building.

Chapter Two

Altitude Chamber

Our crew is off duty the next day, and then it's back to ground sessions. At the Ops Building, the schedule board tells me that Panetta and I are scheduled for a half-day celestial review class at the Link Training Building. Also posted on the scheduling board is information for our next flight—and, finally, they have posted the date for our deployment to Guam.

We had been told that we would have about twenty days' notice of the trip to Guam. The squadron knew that the date was getting close, but today we find the first official notice on the board. The 40th Bomb Squadron will be departing Walker AFB on 12 September for three-month rotation duty in Guam. Firm notice about the deployment stirs up a constant buzz in Flight Ops. We all have personal plans and obligations of all kinds that will need to be adjusted.

At 1215 hours, quiet conversation fills the small classroom at the Link Trainer Building, used for celestial training. The class is made up of twelve navigators and five observers from the three squadrons. Most of the buzz is about Guam. Lieutenant Colonel Colby enters the classroom, and we all rise from our chairs as he sets his books down, looks up, and then nods for us to sit again.

"We will be covering a quick review of the sextant, use of the dome, finding and selecting celestial targets, computations, use of the star and sun tables, and plotting fixes. You all know the material, and this review is to shake out any bad habits that have taken hold and to clean up any procedures that may have become sloppy.

"Most important is to practice finding those constellations and target stars that you seldom use in flight. We all have our favorites, but when you are faced with partial cloud cover and your old standby targets are not available, you will need to find other stars you can use and you won't have time to fumble with research. You don't want to find yourself standing at the dome in a panic because you can't find a target you can use and you need a celestial fix right now. As always, at the end of the class, you will be tested and scored on finding and identifying constellations and target stars."

Lieutenant Colonel Colby is navigator on the 39th Squadron Select Crew. Each squadron has one "Select Crew," determined by overall scores in bombing, radar, radio, engineering, navigation, gunnery, and procedures related to special weapons. Colby's rank is actually major, but he and each member of the Select Crew hold a spot promotion of one rank higher as long as they remain Select.

"If you have a question, raise your hand," Colby says. "Questions are important and need to be answered right away, not at the next break."

The information comes at us pretty fast, slowed down only by questions and requests to explain or repeat a particular point.

I sure need this, I think. *Some of these target stars I haven't used since navigation school.*

Panetta and I will be shooting these other target stars in the future, even though the familiar ones are available.

At 1815, we are just finishing.

Colonel Colby sums up: "You have identified cloud-obscured constellations, what quadrant of the sky to find them, and the important target stars. You have exchanged answer sheets and reviewed them, and have your own answer sheets back. Prior to your next flight, you will work on any areas of weakness and shape up. That might save you some night from shitting in your pants when your AC asks for your position while you are over the middle of the Pacific, have 50 percent cloud cover above obscuring your favorite target stars, and have had no fixes for the last hour. Any questions? No? Have a good evening, gentlemen."

We stand as Colonel Colby leaves the classroom.

* * * * *

The next afternoon, the Squadron Board shows that our full crew is scheduled for the altitude chamber at 0800 the next day—and that's an all-day drill. We're scheduled for class in the morning and then an actual session in the chamber after lunch.

I find Major Kingby at a desk in the briefing room. He looks up over the pile of papers he's working on and I catch his eye.

"Major Kingby, looks like we will be at altitude chamber all day tomorrow."

"Sounds about right," he replies.

"Anything I need to be doing the rest of this afternoon?"

"Nothing. Go on and take the rest of the day off." He sighs. "I hope that I can get through this stack before 0800 tomorrow morning and have a beer myself at some point."

"Thank you, sir," I say and retreat quickly.

The major grunts, adjusts his glasses, and looks down at his papers. I step out into the sunshine, pass through the flight line gate, and then head two blocks to the O Club for a drink and something to eat. I find Major Heller and Captain Cruz already at the bar with a beer in hand and no thoughts about having any food for a while.

* * * * *

The next morning, I get myself a breakfast from the buffet line in the O Club, scooping up my favorite breakfast of mixed fruit, scrambled eggs, sausage, and hash browns. My way to start the day. I'm at the Altitude Building at 0740 hours, ready to go. The Altitude Building stands alone, and is small in area but is twenty feet high. Entrance is directly into the classroom. Through a large glass window in one wall of the classroom, I can see the pressure chamber itself filling up most of the space in the next room. The only other rooms in the building are two offices and a toilet.

The chamber in the adjoining room is properly called the "Altitude Decompression Chamber." It is an intimidating cylinder of thick steel, about ten feet in diameter and thirty feet long, painted a forbidding dark gray. The sections of the cylinder are joined together by heavy continuous welds. On the near side of the cylinder is a row of small thick-glass viewports about six inches in diameter and spaced about three feet apart, running the full thirty feet of the tube. Thick steel brackets are embedded every four feet into the concrete floor of the building, and the cylinder is welded to the brackets with heavy-duty welds. Welded at each end of the cylinder is a ten-foot-diameter steel end plate, bowed out at the center. From the classroom, the whole cylinder looks like part of a primitive submarine.

Master Sergeant Greene is our instructor for the class. He looks about forty years old, six-foot-two—a black man who looks like he spends a lot of time lifting weights. He is obviously career Air Force, and don't you forget it. Over a three-hour period, he covers all of the technical aspects of an aircraft at high altitude, oxygen systems on the B-36, oxygen masks, and walk-around bottles. When he entered the classroom, he carried a thick black loose-leaf reference book that he then set down on the lectern. But the sergeant never opened the reference book to refresh his memory or check a fact during the entire three-hour class. He didn't need to. Sergeant Greene reviewed the effects on the human body deprived of sufficient oxygen at various altitudes, symptoms of oxygen loss, and many associated facts and information. I was amazed at his knowledge, clarity, and logical presentation. He answered all our questions. No problem.

We break for lunch and then our crew returns to the Altitude Building, all having changed into flight suits as we were instructed to do. We move out of the classroom and into the big room housing the chamber itself.

Master Sergeant Blake waves at us to gather around. "I am Chief Master Sergeant Blake, in charge of this facility. Welcome. Our team is made up of NCOs trained and experienced in this special operation. Senior Master Sergeant Turner will be giving directions and instructions while you are in the chamber, and the voice you hear will be his. In the chamber with you will be two master sergeants to observe, assist, and instruct as needed, and outside the chamber are stationed eight tech and staff sergeants who will observe you through the ports. Please step around to the other side of the chamber and we will begin."

As we walk around the tank, I can see the business side of the chamber. Ducts, pipes, tubes, and wires penetrate the steel shell. I can hear the low hiss of pressured air venting. This length of the cylinder has a row of small glass ports, same as the other side. At one end of the cylinder is a free-standing control panel with a number of gauges, controls, switches, and colored lights arranged in orderly patterns. A young tech sergeant stands by the panel waiting, almost at parade rest.

At the center of the long side of the tank is a small, heavy-hinged entrance door standing open with a metal grate ramp up to the door sill. Up close, I can feel the enormous size and weight of the tank. Following the man in front of me, I walk up the ramp and step over the raised curb. I feel a cold sweat on my back as we enter the forbidding tank. I become well aware that there is only one way out of the chamber and that is through the door we are now passing through. I'm beginning to feel a little confined already.

On each side of the tank sits a wooden bench almost the full length of the tube, with wide yellow stripes painted on the bench and dividing it into stations. Bright tube lights line the center of the ceiling. Over the bench at each station is a panel, with a connected oxygen mask, air pressure gauge, valve, and colored lights. Cool air circulates through the space, and even though my armpits and forehead are still sweaty from anxiety, the sweat is now cool and wet. The air has a strong machine taste and smell.

Maybe I should have taken a piss when we got back from lunch and before getting into this steel pipe. Too late now …

At each end of the chamber stands a master sergeant, relaxed and casual, oxygen mask and panel near his head and three walk-around bottles at his side. The only sounds I can hear are shuffling of boots, controlled escaping air pressure, and the deep breathing of the crew members. There is no elevator music provided to sooth the nerves.

A damned-over controlled situation if I ever saw one. No conversation because no one has anything to say. We file in, sit, and look across at the man on the opposite bench. I can taste my lunch again. Not much eye contact among the crew members.

Do all the flight crews take a ride in this damn steel pipe—and today we are the randomly chosen few? I sigh. *Nothing is random in this Air Force.*

The entrance door slams shut, and I can hear the steel door dogs being locked into place.

31

I reach for my standard "escape" thinking. I concentrate on standing on the top of a ski run at Mammoth Ski Area, breathing deeply, set to start a downhill run. Sunny sky, clean white snow, skiers dressed in brightly colored jackets and hats swishing down the slope. I can almost see groups of skiers at the bottom of the hill, animated and smiling, clustered around the ski lifts and lodge building.

The calm voice of Sergeant Turner interrupts my escape and his voice fills the space: "Welcome, gentlemen. Please raise your hand if you have been lucky enough to have experienced this exercise before. We're starting our ascent."

Two hands are raised. Turner nods his head to acknowledge the raised hands.

The hiss of air pressure grows louder. They are sucking air pressure out of the tank to bring us to altitude.

Sergeant Turner's monologue continues: "Partner up with the man on your left or right. Keep an eye on each other. During this exercise, if you feel distressed, have a problem, or need to communicate with staff, raise your hand."

He reviews in detail the symptoms and effects on the body from insufficient oxygen. The sergeant also covers how best to restore oxygen to a crew member in trouble, what to look for, and the action to take if you sense yourself lacking oxygen.

"We are passing through 10,000 feet," he continues. "As you all know, oxygen is required above 10,000 feet. Put your mask on, and check your mask and air tube. Check your partner's equipment also. Staff will be monitoring you all as we ascend. Note your own reactions to the changes in altitude and oxygen flow."

Silence. I hear muffled breathing sounds and that's all that I hear. I look at the eyes of the man across the tank. Everyone is serious as hell and thinking only about altitude and oxygen. The constantly moving eyes of each of the staff members check us out as we ascend.

When we are in flight, I have my mask on at high altitude, and suck in oxygen without thinking much about it because I'm busy doing my job. The mask is annoying, and my own breathing sounds loud and rasping, even with my headset in place. I don't have time to think about it. At altitude, the heavy cold-weather clothing and oxygen mask make the job more difficult and I need to concentrate more on getting the job done, not on the oxygen mask.

The two sergeants are now standing in the aisle. Turner tells us that we are now at 25,000 feet and gives instructions. One crew member of each pair is to remove his mask. My turn first, and I unbuckle the strap from around my head and let the mask drop down.

I tell my partner, "Everything is okay. Normal."

A few breaths later, I feel a little lightheaded and turn to my partner to tell him so, but the words come out as a slur and I feel stupid. My eyes water up, and my breathing rate increases as my body searches for air. I look at my partner, but he is a little out of focus. I raise my hand to my face, but miss and graze my ear.

My partner jams my mask back onto my face and holds it there. My rapid breathing slows as I suck in oxygen. Tastes metallic. After a minute, my eyes clear and I strap on my mask. My partner looks concerned, so I give him a thumbs-up and ignore my headache.

Two minutes later, Lieutenant Perez, my partner, reluctantly removes his mask. He looks at me, anticipating what is going to happen. After a minute, his eyes widen and water up. He gets a half-smile on his face and starts breathing rapidly. Perez's eyelids begin to droop as I watch—and then I remember that I'm supposed to give him his mask. The sergeant is moving toward us as I quickly press Perez's mask to his face. The sergeant stands close, looks down at us, and just watches. I look at the sergeant's eyes over his mask and they tell me I was late with the mask. Perez looks better but he isn't happy. Perez places one of his hands over mine on his mask and then straps on the mask with his other hand. We both let go of the mask and he nods okay.

Turner's voice again: "We are climbing to 40,000 feet. I will tell you when we are there. Any problems, let us know."

All is calm. The sounds of my own breathing and the hissing air are all I hear. I guess a few minutes pass.

"We are at 40,000 feet and will remain at this altitude for two minutes and then slowly descend," Turner says. "This is the boring part."

We all sit in silence. We are descending from altitude and I clear my ears twice. I'm tired and would like to get out of this steel tube. I listen my own labored breathing. I think that we are still descending slowly, but I have no way to know our chamber altitude.

"We are at 20,000 feet," Turner calls out.

BOOM!

An explosion …

The air becomes foggy and damp and I am breathing too fast. My eardrums snap and I feel a sharp pain in both ears. The in-cabin instructors are standing in the aisle, checking every face.

The sound system speaks: "You have just experienced a simulated explosive decompression in flight at 20,000 feet. You may now remove your masks."

An instructor presses an olive-drab towel under my nose as I remove my mask. I look down past his hand and see blood on the front of my flight suit.

Must be my blood. That's odd.

A little bit of liquid in my mouth tastes warm and metallic. Everything tastes metallic. Don't feel like I'm bleeding. I look up at the sergeant.

He smiles. "Just got yourself a little nosebleed," he says and motions me to take hold of the bloody towel that he is still holding.

I grab the towel and now I have a good-sized headache. The instructor disconnects my oxygen hose and bloody mask, and wraps them in another towel. I can see a red mess on my flight suit, and then I look up to meet the eyes of everyone else looking at me. I shrug my shoulders to signal an apology, since it looks as if I'm the only guy with blood dripping down the front of his flight suit.

"What a mess," I mutter with the towel still under my nose and over my mouth.

Embarrassing …

We all file slowly out of the chamber, and I still have the towel at my face. I look for the toilet.

A voice rings out: "Lieutenant Hall, telephone."

I look up and see one of the younger instructors holding part of a phone up in the air and looking at me. As I come close, the sergeant holding the phone says, "Flight surgeon," and hands me the phone. Someone has obviously called the base hospital. I imagine that any incident in the chamber, if at all medical, needs to be called in to the hospital, to record and request instructions—even just a nosebleed.

A voice on the phone asks, "This is Colonel Becker, flight surgeon at the hospital. Got yourself a nosebleed? How are you feeling?"

34

"Bleeding has about stopped," I reply. "Got myself a headache now but otherwise okay, sir."

"Headache should be gone by morning. Call the hospital if the headache persists or you have any other problems."

"Yes, sir."

Click.

We're done.

* * * * *

On Thursday morning, I walk to the gate in the fence at the flight line, hold up my flight pass to the Air Police at the gate, and say, "Good morning."

No response, which is a little unusual. I look toward the Flight Line Building, where eight or ten men are standing and talking near the door to the building. Something is going on.

I walk to one of the groups and ask, "Charlie, what's happening?"

Charlie quietly responds, "One of the planes from the 39th Squadron went down last night."

"Shit," I said. "What do we know?"

The 6th Bomb Wing has lost two aircraft within a couple of weeks. The wing had lost none before that since I've been stationed at Walker.

"Major Hendrick and his crew were up last night on a routine fourteen-hour flight. Over Texas, the plane broke up at 24,000 feet and went down. It burned when it hit the ground."

"What do you mean 'broke up'? B-36's don't just break up in flight."

"The story that I heard is that the plane flew, without warning, into a tornado forming at altitude," Charlie said. "Wind shear snapped off the left wing up to engine number two. The plane must have done a wingover and been so out of control that no one could get out. The jets were not online, and it went nose down and burned."

I have never thought very much about that part of the scene. B-36's routinely shut down engines in flight because of overheating or loss of oil, or sometimes an engine fire. I've heard of an aircraft landing with three engines out, but not very often. With any significant engine problems, pilots bring the jets online, and the jets then provide enough additional power to make an emergency landing. If a plane were at 40,000 feet, the jet engines would already be online and powered up. At 24,000 feet, with no bomb bay load, the jets were probably offline. Would have made no difference anyway, with the half of the left wing gone.

We all knew that B-36's had crashed in the past two years, but their loss was never reported in the newspapers or on TV, and not discussed publicly on base. I'm sure the bigwigs investigate every incident until they know the how and why, but the rest of us don't have a need to know.

Colonel Romeo turns from another group standing at the flight line building and looks at us. He's an aircraft commander, has flown B-29's, and had a tour in Korea before being assigned to SAC and B-36's. Most of the younger crew members, including me, have never faced combat, and all the experience we have is in the B-36 and Strategic Air Command. For a minute, Romeo listens to our comments of surprise and shock.

He steps closer to our group and says, "Did you think this flying business is a free ride? You are the best of the best, so you've been assigned to Strategic Air Command to fly in our B-36's. Our Air Force squadrons of B-36 aircraft are our Cold War shield, and SAC wants the best men we have to be part of that shield. It has priority and SAC will not release you for other duty. You men are being held back and out of the Korea mess. Hope our shield is never ordered into combat. We are the only military system the United States has right now that can drop a nuclear weapon on any enemy. Army and Navy do not yet have that capability. Air Force aircraft crews go down every day all over the world, so don't be so damned shocked. Keep all that in mind and do your job."

He walked off, looking down at his boots.

In flight, one of the duties of the radar officer is to watch for weather showing up on the scope. Did the weather not show? Was Radar asleep? Did Radar not recognize the pattern? Maybe the brass would know after their investigation. Maybe not. We in the trenches would never find out and the incident would not be discussed, but I hope that we would all benefit from whatever is learned from the investigation.

The memorial service for the entire crew takes place in the largest chapel on base on Tuesday at 0800 hours. Every man is dressed in his Class A uniform. The chapel is full, including the aisles. There are about fifty of us who can't get in the chapel and can't hear the service, but we stand silently just outside as if we are within the chapel until the service ends. Only one casket holds the remains of the entire crew, and that casket will stay in the chapel with an honor guard of two Air Force military police until sundown.

The next day, Wednesday, is a full workday in muted tones.

* * * * *

That same day, a notice is posted on the Squadron Board:

40ᵗʰ BOMB SQUADRON:

WE WILL BE TDY GUAM 12 SEPT 54 FOR APPROX. 90 DAYS. THIS TDY WILL NOT ALLOW THE SQUADRON TO COMPLETE OUR NORMAL TRAINING SCHEDULE WHILE DEPLOYED. THEREFORE BETWEEN NOW AND THE DATE THAT WE DEPLOY, THE 40ᵗʰ SQUADRON WILL BE SCHEDULED FOR AND COMPLETE CURRENT TRAINING REQUIREMENTS PLUS TRAINING THAT WOULD NORMALLY TAKE PLACE DURING DEPLOYMENT. ANY REQUIRED TRAINING NOT COMPLETED BEFORE TDY WILL BE COMPLETED AFTER TDY, ALONG WITH ROUTINE TRAINING SCHEDULED FOR THAT PERIOD.

T. S. NAGEL, COLONEL
40ᵗʰ BOMB SQUADRON

Alongside that notice hangs the schedule for survival training at Stead Air Force Base in Nevada.

"Can't be!" I nearly shout.

The schedule shows that I am assigned to a summer session of Survival School for twelve days, beginning 15 August 54. I will return from Stead about two weeks before leaving for Guam!

"Impossible," I mutter.

The guy looking over my left shoulder at the notice now chuckles. I'm sure he is overjoyed that my name is on the schedule rather than his. I spin around and head for the Operations office.

The master sergeant who runs the office for the Operations Officer sees me approaching and knows what is on my mind. He smiles and says, "How can I help you, Lieutenant Hall?"

"Master Sergeant, your office has me scheduled for Stead starting 15 August."

Still smiling, he says, "Yes, I know. We've put together a crew departing that date."

"Can't be!" I say. "I was just at Stead in November last year and completed Winter Survival. Check out the paperwork."

I am feeling warm all over, trying to stay calm as I remember all that damn snow and eating out of a #10 steel can that once held beets.

"I know, Lieutenant Hall, middle of November. November was Winter Survival, I'm sure you recall. You have not completed Summer Survival requirements."

"I'll bet there are thirty or forty people in this squadron who haven't done summer yet, and I bet they didn't do winter six or seven months ago."

"You might be right," the sergeant says, "but the major, in all his wisdom, decided that you are unmarried, in fine physical shape, and you seem to be in stable mental condition. He said you are just the man to fill this slot and complete your Summer at Stead next month."

"He probably doesn't want to send one of his potbellied forty-five-year-old crewmen," I say. "Let's hope that none of the old men have to try to walk out of the USSR someday."

I glare at the sergeant, who is still smiling. Then I lift my arms up in the air in surrender, back away, and have to grimace at my bad luck. The master sergeant with the big potbelly is still smiling.

Looks like I'm going to be busy right up to the departure date for Guam. Guess that's what they keep lieutenants around for: to fill holes in rosters for duty like Survival School!

Chapter Three

Albuquerque Station

It is Friday morning, almost 0800 hours, and I open the door to the lobby of the building with a small sign on it reading: *Library Center.* The Library Center is located on the flight line, ten feet from the fence that separates the flight line from the rest of the base. This building has its own guarded gate through the fence that is used only by people who have business at the Library Center.

Standing in the lobby are two of our crew, wearing Class A uniforms instead of flight suits, as we have all been instructed to wear by Major Kingby. They are talking quietly. I make eye contact and give them a "Good morning, gentlemen." Waiting are Captain Harris, second pilot, and Captain Cruz, our first engineer, and they respond with a lackluster morning greeting. I get the impression that they are not very happy to be here. I join them, and at 0800, Major Kingby and Major Heller complete our group.

"Good morning," Kingby says.

"Good morning, sir," we chorus back.

Major Kingby walks by us and opens the door to the main room of the building. Just inside that door, we each have our photo ID checked by an Air Force police noncom and then file into the library.

The library is a fairly large space. The left side of the room is filled with shelving from floor to the ceiling, holding hundreds of gray files. The shelving and files extend almost the full length of the room. A counter separates the file stacks from about ten tables, each with six chairs.

Some of the tables are occupied, and Major Kingby is directed by one of the library staff to an empty table that has been assigned to our crew, and we all follow. In the middle of the table are three stacks of files waiting for us.

This is the first time I have been in this building. Those at the occupied tables have files spread all over the work tops and are talking quietly, reading and comparing information. The room is well lit, and the hum of the air-conditioning equipment masks the quiet talk from the occupants of the tables.

Here is where B-36 crews study data, intelligence photos, and information about the targets that we have been assigned to destroy with a special weapon if so ordered. The mood in the room is quiet, somber, and serious. Major Kingby pulls one of the three stacks of files toward him, reads the tab on each file, and hands it off to the appropriate crew member, doing the same for the other two stacks of files.

In the navigator file, I find charts, along with photos probably taken from a high-flying reconnaissance plane, plus planned routes, altitudes, and no-wind estimated times for each leg of the flight. A photo of the target city, taken from a very high altitude, looks useless to me. It belongs in radar's file. At our planned altitude over the Initial Point and the bomb run, and with the possibility of cloud decks below, I doubt that I would ever have an opportunity to see the target as it is shown in the photograph. The photo is taken from directly over the target. By the time we are directly over a target, Radar is in control of the aircraft. I would be sitting at my station with my hands on my table, waiting. I would have already navigated the aircraft to the Initial Point and would be sitting, rigid with fear, waiting for release of the weapon.

The plan, as outlined in the files at the library, is to fly a first leg from Walker AFB to Guam, a weapon storage field where a nuclear weapon will be loaded into the bomb bay of our aircraft. Since Guam is not only a weapon storage facility but also our prestrike base, we will remain at Guam to refuel and wait for orders. The wait time will be unknown: maybe hours, maybe days, maybe weeks. What we will be waiting for are orders to strike. The next leg is the long one, the combat flight itself, which will end with our crew releasing a weapon on our previously assigned target. On this leg, we know that we are being tracked by enemy radar. Our aircraft will change direction often to try to confuse the enemy trackers as long as possible about the identity of our assigned target. The last leg, after bomb drop, is to a designated airfield in friendly territory.

The scope of all this feels mind deadening. I study files and maps to the primary and alternate targets.

How many people live in our target city? Would the order to go be absolutely necessary? Would their bombers assigned with targets in the United States already be in the air when we take off? After the drop, will there be an airfield for us to land on in friendly territory that has not already been destroyed by our enemy? I will have orders but no other information to factor in. Insane.

We study. Anyone else harboring questions like these? I don't know.

The conversations tapers off.

Major Kingby speaks softly: "Anyone not finished reviewing the files?"

No response.

"Anyone with questions?"

No response.

"We're done. All files to the center of the table. Three stacks."

We wait while Major Kingby completes and signs a blue-colored form. He tears out his copy, folds it, and shoves it into his pocket. The original he places atop the files, then rises and heads for the door. We follow.

At the door, he turns and speaks to all of us in a very quiet, very tense voice: "As you know, we keep our mouths shut forever about this goddamn library. I will see you all at the flight line building at 1300 hours this afternoon."

"Goddamn?" Man, Kingby is really pissed off. He never says "goddamn." Wonder what he's thinking? The nuclear bomb? The target? The people? The responsibility? Don't know. No one is going to be talking about this "goddamn library" once we leave this building. I sigh. So be it.

We will be scheduled for a morning at the library every eight months, or sooner if world craziness demands it.

* * * * *

The bulletin board at the flight office orders that all crew gunners report to the gunnery simulator on Tuesday at 0730 hours. Panetta and I, for some reason, are on the list of gunners required to report to the simulator. Training gigs are being scheduled back to back. Some people say that Wing must be working through the night to jam all of these requirements into the days between now and the flight to Guam—and besides that, I've got that damn Survival School the middle of next month.

On Tuesday, Panetta and I are at the gunnery simulator fifteen minutes early. All five gunners from our crew are already there and anxious for class to begin.

I saw Panetta at the O Club bar last night, and we had a few beers. Most of the talk at the bar was about the coming trip to Guam. Neither one of us had ever been there, so the Guam veterans at the bar told us all about the joys and sorrows waiting for us. Lots of laughs, lots of BS, and lots about the gorgeous chocolate-skinned native women of Guam. They said that there were also two hundred nurses stationed at the big Navy hospital at the opposite end of the island from Anderson Air Force Base when they were there. Sure.

The gunners spend a good part of their ground time at the aircraft, cleaning and checking their guns and systems. In addition to the guns themselves, they have to check out and maintain their remote electrically operated firing systems and stations. Part of their responsibilities is to load individual shells into the belts and the belts into the .50-caliber guns. Loading ammunition is a tough and dirty job that has to be done before every flight. If their flight requirements included firing all guns, then they have some real fun. When firing out at altitude is part of their requirements on a flight, they have to expend all their ammo and are scored on how many shells remained unfired. Unfired shells indicate that their weapon jammed or shells were misaligned in the load belts, or something else. For the gunners, the simulator is 100 percent fun after a half-hour of classroom time.

For Panetta and myself, the session is a joke.

"We don't have any guns up front," Panetta said. "What are we doing here?"

Tech Sergeant Gordon, our tail gunner, responds, "Early models of the B-36 had a pair of .50-caliber guns mounted at the clear dome at the nose of the aircraft and had a remote firing station next to the navigator. The observer was the primary gunner and the navigator was the alternate. At that time, no nation, including ours, had an interceptor that could climb to our 40,000-foot bomb-run altitude, so all the guns on board were just insurance."

"So why were the nose guns taken out?" Panetta asks.

"Eighteen months later," Gordon says, "both the USSR and we had interceptors in the air that were effective at 40,000 feet and we lost our protection of altitude. The plane builders were told to stop mounting guns in the nose. What I heard was that chances of an interceptor approaching head-on with a B-36 bomber, giving a closing speed of 800 or 900 miles per hour, were none. We're a much bigger and easier target from above or below, so the nose guns were removed."

"So now," Panetta says, "my question is, what are Hall and I doing at gunnery simulator?"

A couple of the gunners who have been listening to the conversation laugh out loud.

Gordon smiles and says, "I believe, but I may be wrong, that the B-36 had its guns removed from the nose, but gunnery training for navigators and observers was never removed and is still in the manuals. That's why you are here. Six months later, interceptors, both ours and the USSR's, started carrying missiles, and they could stand back two or three miles and take us down, well out of range of our guns. We still needed scanners in the aft compartment, and maybe the tail gunner could still provide effective fire, so all the gunnery systems were kept. That's why we gunners are still drawing flight pay."

The gunners all log time in the simulators, comparing scores and trading barbs, thoroughly enjoying themselves. Firing out a full load with no shells to be belted and no guns to clean is just a game. Panetta and I hang back and watch, enjoying the scene. As we walk from the building after the gunnery session is complete, I tell Panetta I've read that since B-36 aircraft are now so vulnerable, SAC is developing a featherweight B-36 configuration. It is stripped of all guns and everything else not absolutely necessary to deliver the weapon. The plane has a crew of six, made up of an engineer, navigator, radar, radio, and two pilots. Some of SAC's squadrons are already in training to fly the featherweight configuration.

Delivery contour for the featherweight, when in range of hostile aircraft, would be to fly under radar detection a few hundred feet above terrain. When near the target, the B-36 would nose up, almost vertical, to a preplanned altitude, then release so that the weapon would continue vertical for a short time, before it loops over and noses down onto the target. The B-36, upon release of the bomb, would immediately turn away from the target at maximum airspeed to try to avoid the effects of the explosion.

Good luck. Impossible.

Seems to me that the featherweight B-36 is the last desperate attempt to make use of the aircraft while waiting for enough B-52's to become operational and replace the B-36. I do not believe SAC expects anyone to survive that bomb-release scenario, but the weapon would be delivered and that's what counts.

Panetta had joined our crew about five months ago, direct from Observer School. He received his commission through AROTC in college and requested flight school. He completed Cadet Training and Nav/Obs School about six months after I did and was also assigned directly to the 6th Bomb Wing at Walker AFB.

We buy each other a beer at the O Club Bar quite often and are comfortable talking to each other. Paul told me once that his parents sailed to the United States from Naples, Italy, and then traveled to Ohio with the promise of jobs. Paul's father was learning to cut hair in Naples, so he was able to get a job in a barber shop and eventually earned a license to be a barber in Ohio.

Panetta, though, has no plans to be career Air Force. The Air Force helped him pay for his education, and he's grateful for that. Paul wants to complete his obligation to the Air Force, then return to civilian life and make use of his degree in civil engineering. He is grateful for the financial help through AROTC and is determined to do his best while in the Air Force. Not a bad plan.

He is one of the good guys, looking forward to finding a job in California after his Air Force tour, finding a woman who loves to cook Italian, and living the American Dream. He probably will sit in a navigator or radar position for a while before his tour is over. He's a good crew mate and beer buddy.

* * * * *

It's Tuesday. I'm sound asleep at the BOQ and the damn alert siren shrieks through the night. I'm suddenly sitting up in bed. My mind is empty, not functioning, and then I'm standing by my bed. Moonlight through the window. Bad taste in my mouth. Siren noise fills the room. Long, long, long, short, short, long, long, long … Damn the noise. I'm awake now … Three longs, two shorts, over and over, screaming at me to immediately report to our Squadron Operations Building on the flight line. *Shit, it's 0400 hours.* I hit the light switch, grab clean clothes, and in seven minutes, I'm at my door in flight suit and jacket, cap and boots, with chart case and flight bag in hand.

I look out my door into the hallway and everyone is moving at double-time. I can hear muffled noises from other rooms and boots stamping down the hall. The whole building is alive. The siren finally shuts down, knowing everyone is definitely awake. My eyes sweep my room as I try to think of what I am forgetting. Nothing. I'm out the door, thumping down the hall and stairs with chart case held out in front of me and flight bag on my shoulder.

Outside, every part of the base is lit up, and carrying my bag and chart case, I trot toward the flight line. Maintenance men and flight crews are all heading for the flight line gates. Blue trucks are moving in all directions, carrying people and boxes, and most of them seem to know where they are going. Bright eyes, somber faces, dulled bodies doing what they need to do. Lights are on in the kitchens, offices, and every supply building on base.

I arrive at the flight line gate and stand at the end of a long line, catching my breath and waiting to be cleared through. The line moves quickly. I clear the gate and then walk as fast as I can to our squadron building. The building is crowded already.

"Morning," I hear. Not "Good morning," but just a hollow "Morning." Everyone is cranked up and there's quiet chatter as the building fills up even more. Flight bags are stacked up in the corners, and more bags are left outside the building on the apron. Chart bags remain in hand.

The door to Colonel Nagel's office opens. The colonel stands in the doorway in his gray flight suit and boots.

In a booming voice, loud enough to be heard throughout the building, he bellows, "Listen up! We have an Exercise Red in motion, full 6th Bomb Wing. Maintenance will provide me with a list of all airworthy aircraft to be assigned to our squadron. All aircraft commanders report immediately to the Operations Office to sign for packets prepared by Wing Staff and the Library Center. Weather briefing for AC and Radar only, here at 0600 hours.

"Squadron Operations will assign an aircraft to each aircraft commander. In the briefing room are clipboards for each crew. Every crew member, officer and enlisted, will sign up and then get the hell out of the way, out of the building to make room for the next man.

"At 0645 hours, each crew, with full gear, will meet with its aircraft commander in separate groups spaced along the area outside of this building for a quick briefing and head count. Look for your aircraft commander. At 0715, every blue vehicle on base will be available to transport crews to assigned aircraft.

"All aircraft will be ready to roll at 0800. The tower will control movement of all aircraft and the takeoff sequence. All food facilities are operating. Get breakfast if you have time. Flight food will be delivered to each aircraft. Good luck and safe flight."

The tension erupts. Everyone is moving and talking. Most head to the briefing room to sign in on the clipboards, and some go to the exit doors to grab breakfast from the mess halls to carry back to the Operations Building. No one forgets a trip to the head. I look at the crowd waiting to get to the clipboards and turn away.

I need to get something to eat. Eating has a low priority right now, but it may be a long time until the next meal. I clear through the flight line gate to get back onto the base. The Officers Club is the closest place to get food, and I hustle over. The dining room is crowded but less hectic than I expected. Doors to the kitchen are wedged open. Men and women dressed in full front aprons over fatigues and wearing plastic gloves are pushing kitchen carts of food through the doors to a row of tables set up in the dining room. Cartons of juice and milk and huge piles of wrapped sandwiches cover most of the tables. Stacks of white paper bags, candy bars, and apples fill the rest of the space.

I hustle up to the tables, pick up a white bag, and fill it with three sandwiches, two juices, an apple, and two Baby Ruth bars. Exit doors are wedged open at the far end of the line of tables.

These people must have starting preparing food at 0400. They are on the ball. I move away from the tables, now crowding up with men in flight suits and boots, and head out the door. Through the flight line gate again, with my chart case in one hand and breakfast in the other.

I still need to sign in on our crew clipboard. The briefing room has quieted down some but is still crowded with people waiting to sign in. Those who have signed in are quickly getting out of the building, looking for breakfast. I stand at the end of a line and set the chart case on the floor between my boots. I hesitate to even let the case out of my hand, but my boots will tell me if it moves. I push the case forward and keep clamping a boot on each side. I keep looking at my watch, wait for the line to move a little, close my eyes, and listen. The time is 0610.

I sign in. I need to find some place to sit and eat, and I need to be out on the ramp at 0645. Plenty of time.

Sitting on a low concrete block wall, I take a few deep breaths and eat my breakfast. On the flight line, I can see trucks around most of the B-36's, with maintenance people in the aircraft, on the ground, and atop the wings, all working at top speed. My wristwatch reads 0620. My mind and body slow.

At 0635, I walk to the front of the Flight Line Building. Crews are gathering in clusters, spaced about thirty feet apart. Air Force trucks, buses, vans, and pickups are waiting just beyond the crews. I don't see Major Kingby or any familiar faces, so I move down the line. Heads turn toward me, and some of the men smile and raise their hand in recognition. The smiles make me feel damn good. The smiles tell me, "Welcome to the team."

I see Major Kingby up ahead and join our crew.

Major Kingby is out in front and barks out, "0645. Answer up." He calls each name and is answered with a "Yes, sir," except for Major Heller.

"Major Heller is picking up last-minute target information," Kingby says.

We can see the major trotting toward us from the Flight Line Building.

When the siren wailed at 0400 this morning, I assumed that this was a drill, but you really never know. The newspapers and the TV barkers, for the past few weeks, have told us of no international events or threats above the usual bluster by the United States and the USSR, but at times, the situation can change very quickly.

* * * * *

I feel lucky that I was assigned directly from Air Cadets to B-36 bombers. The war in Korea is still grinding on. Most of the navigators that I graduated with from Air Cadets were assigned to units already in Korea. Tough duty. The navigator sits up front in the nose of a B-26, map-reading at 200 feet above the deck. In combat, they become the loader for the nose gunner. The B-26's fly north from airfields in South Korea and are assigned to provide ground support, to bomb an assigned target or strafe targets of opportunity, and then turn around and get out. They are under constant fire from enemy ground units the entire flight coming and going.

The downside of flying in the B-36 is that if we ever do fly the combat mission we train for, I believe it would be a one-way ride. I think most of the crew agrees, but no one ever speaks of it.

* * * * *

After Major Kingby completes his roll call, he raises his fist, signaling for us to hold and stay in place. He walks to a waiting flatbed stake truck, talks to the driver, and then to the driver of a second truck before he climbs into that cab. The trucks turn and back up to slowly to our waiting crew. We swing our gear up, climb on board, and ride out toward our assigned B-36. On the flatbed, I squat down alongside Panetta.

"How are you doing, Paul?"

"Not bad," he replies. "Couple of more hours' sleep would be great."

"I could use some help on preflight. I know Heller will need some of your time too. Time is about 0700, and taxi time is at 0800 hours. I think Kingby will give us our charts as soon as we climb off the truck."

"What do you need besides the usual preflight?" Panetta asks.

"Besides your own checklist, please run the preflight check list at the nav station for me," I say. "I need some time to look at the charts and the information from the library. We will get charts from Major Kingby with the flight plan already plotted and some other data. Don't even know where we're going yet."

Panetta gives me his standard answer: "No problem."

The trucks stop, keeping their normal safe distance from the plane. I ease off the truck, move to the nose wheel assembly, and set my bags down in front of me, ready for preloading inspection and instructions. The crew form two lines.

Early morning is the best part of the day. Any noise that breaks the early quiet is isolated, easily identified, familiar, and comfortable. A generator whines, vehicles move across the field in the distance, and I can hear the deep rumble of an aircraft engine starting up.

"Listen up," Kingby says. "I have handouts for Radar, Radio, Engineer, Navigator, and Chief Gunner. On this flight, we will be loading a full-weight dummy weapon and dropping on target. Total flight time will be twenty and one-half hours.

"The aircraft will be climbing to 40,000 feet for the bomb run, so double-check your oxygen equipment as soon as we get aboard. We all know that this is the mission that tells General LeMay whether we can do the job or not. Let's get it right. Any questions? No? We will taxi at 0800 hours. Load up." I pick up my handout from Kingby.

Time is 0715 hours. Kingby is first up the forward ladder and I follow him. The gunners, animated and talking, walk toward the ladder access to the aft compartment with all their gear.

Panetta sits in the seat at the nav table, and I sit on the floor near the greenhouse. I check the charts, log, and other information in the handout from Wing. We will be flying north to Albuquerque Station, load a weapon, and drop it on target over water 300 miles northeast of Miami.

'Least I'll have some time while we are on the ground in Albuquerque to go over this information in the handout again.

Panetta is finished at the nav table and climbs up to the celestial dome to mount and check out the sextant. I take the nav seat, pick my chute, and set it on the floor. I can feel the chute with my left boot and know it is where it belongs. All of the crew, except the first pilot, second pilot, and engineer, wear a chute harness for a chest pack over their flight suits. I am never more than a few feet from my chute, and I know—I always know—where it is. It's my security blanket.

The first and second pilots and the engineer wear full backpacks. They would be the last crewmen out, and they would work right up to exiting, leaving no time to wrestle with a chest pack. The rest of us hope we will have time to find and hook up our chest pack if we need to.

The sun is flooding through the greenhouse now. With few words and an occasional grunt or sigh, each crewman makes ready for the flight. I stretch my arms, grateful that I have room to do so. We rarely fly with a standard crew of fifteen. Many times, we have additional people in the forward cabin. Sometimes they are part of the squadron Select Crew, hovering over us and checking our work; sometimes they are men newly assigned to the B-36 and just observing. With only thirteen on board again, the cabin seems almost spacious.

"Hey, Panetta," I say, "ever been to Miami?"

"Not yet," he answers.

"Well, today's the day. We are going to Miami."

We are ready to roll at 0800, but are in line behind two B-36's already on the taxiway. We wait and use the time to double-check everything to make sure that we're ready for takeoff. Our aircraft is wheels up at 0822. I return to my station from the radio room and log in our takeoff time.

* * * * *

The time is 0905, and we start our descent into Albuquerque Station. The flight was about an hour long to get to Albuquerque. The field is located about fifty miles from everywhere and nowhere. Looking out of the greenhouse window, Albuquerque Station looks pretty forlorn, sitting on the high desert all by itself.

"Bob," I say to Major Heller, "have you ever been to Albuquerque Station?"

"Once before, about three years ago. Not one of my favorite places," Heller says.

As we fly lower, I can see that a chain-link fence surrounds the entire facility and looks higher than usual, with rolled barbwire atop its full length. Guard towers are spaced along the entire fence, and outside the fence is a wide swath of plowed fields and then another chain-link fence beyond. *Looks like a prison to me.* I imagine there are mine fields, detectors, and cameras in that plowed strip.

On the side of the runway that is opposite to the support buildings sits a large concrete aircraft parking area. The area is connected to the runway by four taxiways. Beyond the parking area is a row of large concrete-block buildings, with wide spaces between them. Through broken clouds below, we descend into our approach pattern.

* * * * *

As we drop down to our landing-pattern altitude, I can see neat orderly rows of dozens of B-36 aircraft on the sprawling concrete apron. Men swarm around every plane, and support vehicles fill the spaces between aircraft.

Tractors pull trailers loaded with dummy Big Boys, easily identified as first-generation atomic bombs by their grotesque size and shape. Four aircraft are stacked up near the end of the runway, waiting for takeoff. There are three planes in front of us in the landing pattern, waiting their turn to land.

After waiting our turn, landing goes off as normal, and after rumbling over what seems like miles of taxiway, our aircraft reaches our assigned spot on the apron. We park alongside four aircraft, each of them with a group of ground personnel working under open bomb bay doors.

As soon as our engines stop, Major Kingby tells us that we will be on the ground about ninety minutes.

"Transportation is standing by," he says. "You can leave all your equipment on the aircraft. A bus will take us to the crew building to wait while the bomb bay is loaded."

Ground crew vehicles are already approaching our open bomb bay doors. Major Heller and his backup for weapons control, third pilot Lieutenant Perez, stay with the aircraft to observe weapon loading. The rest of us climb onto the bus and are transported to the crew building to wait. I pick up two sandwiches and a coffee from a table in the crowded room, eat my sandwiches, and watch as waiting crew members sit quietly, read, or try to sleep.

Major Kingby, in response to a question from Panetta, tells us that Albuquerque Station is a storage and loading facility. Its only purpose is to stockpile combat and dummy nuclear weapons, and load them onto aircraft when ordered to do so.

From the crew building, we can see ramps that go below grade under the buildings. Air Police patrol around the buildings and the areas around the B-36's being loaded.

Major Kingby says, "The buildings you see store the practice weapons. Underground are the combat weapons. Hope we are never here loading weapons from below."

* * * * *

I hitch a ride in a passing pickup truck to get back to the aircraft and get a closer look at the loading operation. Activity around the aircraft is at high speed but controlled. Exercise Red puts everyone under the gun to perform, and teams of officers in flight suits are watching closely and timing everyone while they do their job. Armament men sweat in the bomb bay, setting up to receive our weapon, and Heller is up close, watching. The work being done is an armament specialty, too detailed for Heller to know exactly the procedures, but he is watching intently. As is often the case in the military, he is relying on others to do the work properly, but Heller will be signing off and will be held responsible.

Refueling is in process, and some minor maintenance on engine number two is just starting. Two men, stripped to the waist in the hot New Mexico sun, stand on a yellow scissor platform high in the air, removing the cowling from the underside of engine number two. The blond-haired kid's sweaty skin is so tanned, it looks almost as dark as the shiny skin of the black man working alongside him. Of course, both men wear Air Force-issue pilot's sunglasses. Recruiting poster material in motion.

We are scheduled for takeoff at 1315 hours. I sit in the shade under a wing with my back against one of the nose wheels. It is about an hour before takeoff. I lean my head back against the wheel and doze off in spite of the heat, noise, and activity around me. It is going to be a long flight before we touch down again at Walker.

Chapter Four

Miami/Walker

Our takeoff is late. While we wait in line at the end of the runway, number two engine on the B-36 just in front of us starts spewing black smoke. The pilot of the aircraft in front of us shuts down his engine number two and continues to hold his place in line. When he reaches the runway, he taxis wearily onto the runway and turns off at the first taxiway to return to the parking apron.

Even on an Exercise Red, no pilot with one engine down will attempt a takeoff with a full load of fuel and the weight of a weapon on board. The dummy weapon, by design, weighs the same as the combat weapon.

We finally reach the end of the runway, line up, and our people on the flight deck power up all engines. Our takeoff roll starts slowly, and we rumble on the runway a long time before lifting off. We added a lot of weight at Albuquerque. I log takeoff at 1123 hours.

"Navigator to Pilot."

"Pilot here."

"Navigator. Heading to Oklahoma City zero eight two degrees. ETA 1352 hours."

"Pilot, understand zero eight two degrees, Oklahoma City."

We are now carrying a practice bomb in bomb bay number one. The atomic bomb targeting Nagasaki, Japan, in August 1945 was called "Fat Man." It weighed 10,000 pounds and had a yield of 16 kilotons, equivalent to 16,000 tons of TNT. The practice bomb we carry is about the same size and weight as a Mark 6, which is an improved version of the original Fat Man.

Since 1945, the United States has developed atomic bombs that are smaller and lighter than the Mark 6, with much greater yield, and hydrogen bombs with yields measured in megatons, not kilotons.

I'm sure that the flight deck is well aware of the weight of the bomb bay load by the change in performance of the plane, but on the lower deck, I can feel no difference once we are airborne.

At 22,000 feet, we have about 50 percent cloud coverage below and clear skies above. Panetta and I take celestial readings of the sun about every thirty minutes and map-read through the partial cloud deck below.

We are over Oklahoma City at 1358 hours. Panetta relieves me as we turn and head for Atlanta, Georgia.

"How are you doing, Bob?" I call to Radar.

Since climbing on board, Heller has been checking his radar equipment and notes. His bright, nervous blue eyes are never still, and his tanned, creased skin reflects many seasons spent outdoors. On the ground, he never tires of talking about his love of hunting and fishing. Exercise Red is not new to him, but the challenge excites him and the responsibility surely makes him nervous.

"Okay," he responds. "Just checking the manual on the weapon again."

Major Heller likes to call the monster bomb "the weapon." The rest of us usually refer to it as just "the bomb." Heller has prime responsibility for checking out "the weapon" from the time it is loaded in the bomb bay until releasing it on the target. He has adequate reason to be nervous.

It's time to arm the bomb. The dummy nuclear weapon in the bomb bay has, built into its side, all the dials, switches, and toggles that a combat weapon has. Major Heller must now crawl into the bomb bay and prepare the monster by setting and checking all instruments on the casing.

"Radar to Pilot."

"Pilot here."

"This is Radar requesting permission to enter the bomb bay to arm the weapon."

"Radar, you are cleared by Major Kingby to enter the bomb bay. Acknowledge when procedure is completed."

"Will do."

Heller reaches down for a walk-around oxygen bottle and checks the dial to make sure that it is full. He fits the oxygen mask snug to his face, attaches the hose to the mask and checks that he is receiving air. Panetta and I watch as Heller dons gloves and hat. He places an instruction card in his pocket. He knows the instructions as well as his own name but carries the card anyway and also carries a heavy-duty flashlight.

Panetta and I plug in our oxygen masks, check that the masks are working and put on our arctic gloves and hats. Heller heads for the radio room.

"Radio to Engineer."

"This is Engineer."

"Radar is ready to enter bomb bay," says radio.

"Crew, this is Engineer. We will be bringing the forward cabin pressure up to 22,000 feet. Radio and Radar room acknowledge when ready for change in cabin pressure."

"Navigator and Observer ready."

"Radio is ready."

"This is Engineer. Crew on flight deck is ready. Starting decompression now."

My body feels the change in pressure or maybe it's just my imagination. The intercom remains silent. After a few minutes, the engineer calls that the forward cabin is at 22,000 feet altitude. Radio opens the hatch between the radio room and the bomb bay, and Radar crawls through the opening. Radio stations himself at the open hatch, keeping visual contact with Heller. Then Heller crawls on the catwalk about fifteen feet to reach the instrument cluster on the bomb casing.

"Flight Deck, this is Radio. Major Heller is at the bomb panel. All is well."

"This is Pilot. We acknowledge."

All I can hear now is my own breathing and the engine noise. Three long minutes run into four, then silently extend into five.

"Flight Deck, this is Radio. Major Heller is now back in the radio room and the bomb bay hatch is secure."

"Radio, this is Engineer. Understand hatch is secure. Bringing cabin pressure to 9,000 feet."

"Pilot, this is Radar. The weapon is armed."

"Pilot acknowledges that weapon is armed."

After a few minutes, Engineer Cruz informs the crew that the cabin pressure is stable at 9,000 feet. Major Heller moves slowly back to his radar station and we all remove our oxygen masks. His eyes reflect exhaustion as he sets the walk-around bottle down on the floor. Major Heller sits on the floor near his station, pulls up his legs, and rests his arms and head on his knees. After ten minutes, he is back up on his feet and then sits at his station. I sit on the floor in the radar room, eat my sandwiches, and lean back.

"Panetta!" I yell. "Give me thirty minutes."

Paul waves his hand. "Thirty minutes!"

Panetta soon pushes on my shoulder. *Couldn't be a half-hour yet. What's the problem?*

But it is indeed time already, so I tell Panetta, "I'll sit in at the nav table. We've got a long way to go. Get some sleep."

I sit in the navigator position, then check the chart and log. Looks good.

We fly over Atlanta, Georgia, at 1809 hours, and I call the flight deck with a new heading of one five four degrees to Miami, Florida, with an ETA of 2115 hours. Solid cloud layer below and scattered clouds above. Now I am relying solely on star shots, taking sightings about every half-hour.

At 2110, we are over Miami. I call for a new heading of zero five six degrees to take us to the bomb range, located over water 300 miles northeast of Miami.

"This is Major Kingby to crew. All crew members at combat stations and on intercom. Sixty seconds to comply."

Sixty seconds later: "This is Major Kingby. We are at 22,000 feet, with a cabin pressure of 9,000 feet. We will be climbing to 40,000 feet, our altitude for bomb run and weapon release. Get your oxygen masks on now, and check your masks and hose. Weapon release in approximately sixty minutes. All crew members to remain on intercom until we descend from our 40,000 feet bomb run. Chief Gunner, do you read?"

"This is Chief Gunner. I read you and will comply."

"Radio?"

"Radio will comply."

"Radar."

"Radar compartment will comply."

"Engineer?"

"Engineer will comply."

I strap on the damn mask, check my hose, check the walk-around bottle, and then listen to my own breathing. No matter how much I adjust the position of the mask, it seems like it's always in the way. I need to pull in my chin to see the chart over the mask. *Pain in the ass.*

All six engines increase power as we slowly gain altitude. Somewhere in the climb, the flight deck will bring the jet engines online. We're carrying a heavy load.

Flight jacket, stupid, I remind myself.

I quickly remove my earphones, mask, cap, and seat belt, and turn out of my seat to lunge into the radio room for my flight bag. Looks as if everyone else has his flight jacket on. I can feel Sergeant Snell's eyes on me. He is taking note that I forgot to put my flight jacket on before we started our ascent. He's smiling. I can't see his face because of his mask, but I know he is smiling. His eyes are crinkled up in a smile. I smile back, acknowledging my stupidity with an extended middle finger, and he waves back. I put on my jacket, then my seat belt, mask, cap, and earphones.

Major Heller is pressing his face into the eye shield of the radar. I imagine he is bitching to himself about the oxygen mask being in his way.

"Observer, Navigator."

"Observer."

We make eye contact. "We need one more star shot before reaching the Initial Point," I tell him.

"No problem," Paul replies.

He removes his earphones, disconnects his oxygen hose, and plugs into a walk-around bottle. Panetta slowly makes his way through the semidarkness up to the celestial dome, oxygen bottle in one hand and with the other hand grabbing onto whatever he can to steady himself. In the dome, the hose to the bottle is long enough so that he can hold the bottle between his boots. He braces against the aircraft movement and takes sightings on three stars.

Seems like he is up there for a long time, but I know it's just a few minutes and then Panetta is back down, holding the oxygen bottle against his jacket. His breathing is ragged as he hands me a paper showing the observation times and readings.

I plot the fix and call for a small correction to the Initial Point.

Panetta is with Major Heller now. We continue our climb. I can see nothing below except black on black. Jet engines are now at full power. The beast rumbles and whines and continues higher into the dark sky.

"Pilot to Radar."

"Radar here."

"Altitude 40,500 feet. Airspeed three four zero. On course to IP. Acknowledge."

"Radar to Pilot, I acknowledge altitude 40,500 feet, airspeed three four zero and on course to IP."

Silence on the intercom. Engine noise fills the plane.

"Radar to Pilot, over the IP."

Silence again. The pilot drops the right wing and changes heading to bring us on a course to the target.

"Pilot to Radar. Turn complete. On heading to target. You have control."

The pilots take hands and feet off controls. Their hands are on their knees and their feet are flat on the deck. They are sweating and watching the instruments for any sign of a problem. They are not in control and their stress level is over the top. Sweating and watching. Target is a stationary buoy no one can see, but it is sending out a powerful signal. Radar has an image of the target on his scope that is being projected by the target buoy.

"Radar has control," Heller says clearly and calmly.

Panetta is close to Major Heller, peering over his shoulder and checking everything he can see. Only Heller, though, can look into the eyepiece and see the target.

Silence on the intercom. We wait. Engine noises shriek and wail and overwhelm the space. We are at over 40,500 feet, and the vibrations are severe and continuous. I listen to my own labored breathing, look out the greenhouse and still see nothing but black on black.

"Target acquired," Heller says on intercom.

High-altitude winds rock the aircraft, and the radar equipment adjusts automatically, keeping our B-36 on target. Heller is ready to take control if the equipment malfunctions.

More time passes. We wait.

Release … and the aircraft suddenly bounces upward, probably a few hundred feet.

"Bomb away," Radar calls.

He continues to track on his scope, but there is nothing to see except the target blip on the screen. Heller records time of release, and he slumps in his seat and rubs his eyes with both hands.

Suddenly, Major Heller sits up straight in his chair, spins around, and looks across the semi-dark cabin at Panetta and me over his mask. His eyes are red rimmed, stress filled, and tired. He turns back to the green-lit radar, puts his arms on his desk and his head on his arms, and tries to relax.

At "Bomb away," the pilots grabbed the controls and they banked the B-36 sharply left, turning away from the target. Now at 40,500 feet, the plane cannot maintain altitude in the high-speed turn even though all ten engines are still at full power and we are still at bomb-run airspeed. The vibration in our B-36 grows even stronger. We turn 180 degrees toward Miami, losing some altitude but maintaining airspeed. We are running from the target and the bomb as fast as we can.

"Navigator to Pilot."

"Pilot, hold."

The aircraft completes the turn and levels out, still maintaining bomb-run airspeed.

Over the intercom: "Pilot to Navigator, go ahead."

"Navigator to Pilot, heading to Tampa, two five eight degrees."

"Pilot, two five eight degrees to Tampa. Maintaining airspeed to move us away from the drop area, and we are starting our descent."

The weapon has been dropped, but radar is back at his scope. Do the job. Panetta is slumped onto flight bags in the radio room and his eyes are closed. I listen to my own heavy breathing.

* * * * *

Bomb-drop accuracy is measured by mobile scoring units, located on the east coast of Florida for this specific exercise. The units identify each B-36 as it approaches the target and plot the accuracy of its bomb impact. The entire 6th Bomb Wing is bombing that buoy tonight, separated and spaced in flight for safety. After our return to Walker, radar and the aircraft commander of each B-36 will receive a copy of a report from Wing staff stating the accuracy of the bomb drop.

"Pilot to crew, leveling off at 21,000 feet. Airspeed at standard cruise. Cabin pressure at 8,400 feet. Crew off oxygen. All cabins acknowledge."

I immediately climb up for a star fix. Partial cloud cover above. Finally completing the sighting, I twist back down and plot the fix. I call the flight deck with a corrected heading to Tampa, and we are over Tampa at 0014 hours.

When we are over Tampa, I call the flight deck with a new heading to Baton Rouge, Louisiana.

We have been flying over the Gulf since leaving Tampa. I can see an isolated light or two on the water below, probably from fishing boats, but mostly what we see is black. First feet-dry will be at the coast near New Orleans. Panetta comes into the radar compartment, makes eye contact with me and looks almost as tired as I feel ... almost. He raises his hand in surrender and moves forward to the nav seat. I lie down where Panetta had been sleeping on flight bags in the radio room and pull my cap over my face.

Sergeant Snell kicks my boot.

I make eye contact with Snell and ask, "How's it going on the flight deck?"

"Number two had been losing oil for a long time and they shut it down over Tampa. Everything else looks good."

I wave a "Thank you" as I struggle up.

* * * * *

Lou Snell is hunched over his small worktop, writing in his log. The radio operator faces aft with his console mounted on the rear bulkhead of the radio compartment. Black boxes housing electronic and radio components cover the wall. When Snell needs to be away from his radio, he notifies the flight deck and they cover for him. I think he sleeps in his seat, if he sleeps at all. If he lies down to rest, it isn't for very long. Having no second radio on the crew seems to be no problem for Snell.

Sergeant Snell is career Air Force. He was raised in a small town in Texas, where he says men are men and nobody backs down. Lou worked on his father's ranch and still made enough time to finish high school with good grades. His father had been a Marine and had seen combat in the Pacific, and Lou said his father never would answer his questions about combat. Lou enlisted right after high school and his Texas, "Nobody backs down" changed to "It's them against us." For him, it's enlisted men against officers, all the way. The Air Force is pretty relaxed about the distinction between enlisted men and officers, especially in the air—where every crew member, enlisted or officer, has his job. Snell looks down on short-timers, who include everybody not committed to lifetime service. Major Kingby, a career Air Force himself, squashes Snell when he needs it, with just a word and a glare. Snell is married to a pretty gal from Texas who has learned to master Lou's temper and keep him on the straight and narrow path to retirement.

* * * * *

"Paul," I say, "are we due for a fix?"

"Timing is about right."

"I'll take a star reading before I sit in," I tell him.

I'm moving slower now, but still moving. Sky is clear and black, and the target stars jump out at me.

Panetta is still at the nav table. Engine drone is loud but steady, familiar, and almost comforting. I come close and see that he's holding the log in both hands, but his eyes are closed.

"I'll plot the fix," I said.

His eyes snap open. I nudge his shoulder for him to slide out. Panetta hesitates for a second. I don't think he heard what I said, but he says okay anyway and slides out.

The fix looks good. Winds over the Gulf are steady, and our deviation from our planned course is small. No correction.

Major Heller is sitting a little slumped in his seat, head erect, both hands on his table. I can see the back of his head; he's dozing. Nothing much for him to do while we fly over the Gulf, and he hates to give up his radar to Panetta or anyone else.

Every thirty minutes, I read the stars and plot. Time is 0300. I can see a glow from ground lights ahead at eleven o'clock. Should be New Orleans with Baton Rouge a few miles beyond. The night lights of New Orleans are white and yellow with quite a few other colors mixed in. Bars in New Orleans must be open late, and the colors are probably from their neon signs.

Radar is awake and tracking. Major Heller finally gives up his seat, and Panetta gets to have some time on the radar set. Heller is lying down but probably has his wrist alarm set to wake him up often to make sure all is well.

At Baton Rouge, we change heading to two nine zero degrees for the short leg to Dallas, Texas. Sunlight is filtering through behind us. The sun is still below the horizon, but the sky lightens a little. Some stars are still visible, and I take a last star shot as the stars grow dim. Looking aft through the celestial dome, I can see a bit of sun showing above the horizon, pale yellow dulled by ground haze and dust.

Dallas is up ahead, still murky in the haze of dust. Early risers in Dallas must be stirring, and I can see some lights in the city. Bright streaks of yellow flare from over our shoulders and buildings in Dallas reflect the sun.

It is too late to shoot stars and too early for the sun, so I map-read, dead-reckon, and plot. Everyone is stirring and moving. We turn over Dallas to a new heading of two eight zero degrees. We are starting our last leg to Walker, which will be about two and a half hours long.

It is said that this is the most dangerous segment of any flight. "Home-itis" it is called. Pilots know this better than any of us. We are heading home, tired after a long flight, the sun is coming up, and reflexes are slow. Pilots shift in their seats, drink more coffee, and splash water on their faces. Major Kingby steps down from the flight deck and looks in on us.

"Good morning!" he yells above the engine noise and makes eye contact with each of us.

We smile and raise our hands in silent response and he retreats to the radio room. Major Kingby is off the flight deck, with the third pilot at the controls. He is out of his seat to stretch his legs and loosen up. It's his job to land this aircraft, and he is getting himself primed for the task. Kingby lingers in the radio room for a few minutes longer and then climbs back up to the flight deck.

The B-36 starts its slow descent. I am wide awake and have completed my log except for logging in time of landing. Clear skies. I look down at the unyielding monotonous flat, brown high desert and I know that we must be close to home.

"Aircraft Commander to crew. Entering landing pattern. One B-36 ahead of us. Take your positions for landing."

I don't like being in the radio room for takeoffs and landings. If I were in the navigator's seat, I could feel the landing and see the runway coming up to meet us; that would really be something special. I would be closer to the runway than the pilot upstairs, and would be able to look down and almost touch the racing concrete below.

Smooth touchdown. Breaking and reversing engines shove us tight against the radio room forward bulkhead.

Time is almost 0800 hours. Think I'll have a buffet breakfast at the O Club, then sleep forever. Maybe not. Can't go into the club looking and smelling like I do. Maybe a stop at an almost empty diner would be a better idea.

Chapter Five

Water Survival

Today is the first day of August, and the time is 0740 hours. It is already hot outside. Everyone seems to comment that the temperature is high but the humidity is low. *Low humidity? Why are my armpits wet and the headband in my cap damp at 0740 in the morning if we have low humidity?*

Crew is to meet at 0800 in the flight line briefing room. *Wonder what was added to the schedule board during our flight over Miami?*

And ...

Look at that! Nothing new. The staff has been jamming us with training sessions to get ahead before our trip to Guam on 12 September. *They run out of sessions? I still have that damn Survival School on the fifteenth.* And that obligation keeps gnawing at me.

In the briefing room, I sit next to Captain Harris.

"Get any sleep on our flight to Miami?" I ask.

"Yeah, did get some for a change. Kingby decided, I guess, that Greene has had enough sack time lately, and Kingby put him in the left seat with himself in the right. Greene was like a six-year-old with a new toy. He hasn't logged much time in the left seat. He tried to look calm, serious, and professional, but he was so happy, he was ready to piss in his pants. I climbed into the bunk. Greene did well. He's been flying a bunk long enough, and I'm sure he was giddy at the opportunity to finally sit up front."

"I'm sure when he becomes second pilot, he will have fond memories of that sack time long gone," I respond.

Major Kingby stands and faces us. "I know that you are all overjoyed with all the training time we've logged and that the scheduling board shows nothing for us today. Well, this next gig came from Wing Operations directly to me. Tomorrow at 1000 hours we will all meet at the training pool near the parachute rigging building for a bit of water survival training. Dress is dog tags, flight suit with pockets empty, and boots. Bring a second flight suit and boots to change into after your pool time. Anyone who feels he is not physically fit for the pool, come see me as soon as we break up and I'll explain to you why you are. Questions? Good. Dismissed."

We all stand. Sergeant Snell says, "Looks like we'll have good beach weather for tomorrow."

* * * * *

At 1000 hours the next day, I have left my clean flight suit in the locker room and I'm standing at the edge of the pool. The pool is about twenty-five-feet square, utilitarian with concrete decking all around. At one end is a tower, and at the other end, the pool has a ladder at each side. Four instructors, all looking fit and tanned, dressed in OD swim trunks, stand across from us, waiting. Major Kingby had taken a head count and spoken to the master sergeant in charge. The sergeant is dressed in freshly ironed fatigues, not swim trunks.

"Good morning, gentlemen. I am Master Sergeant Burrell. Today we will practice water survival from a ditched plane or from a parachute leap over water. I understand that you may be going on rotation across the Pacific soon, so stay awake."

The sergeant instructs what is expected of us once we step off the tower platform. The five of us closest to the tower put on yellow May West's and a parachute harness for a chest pack.

My turn. The platform looks to be about twenty-five feet above the water, and an instructor stands at the foot of the tower ladder. He looks me in the eye for about three seconds, probably wondering what is going through my mind.

The kid taps me on the shoulder and shows me a fist with his thumb pointed straight up. He jerks his fist up and down a couple of times, and taps me on the shoulder again. The tower is made of wood, but the ladder is aluminum. I climb up and, as instructed, look at the other end of the pool. The instructor told us to look in any direction that we want to but not to look down.

At the platform on top of the ladder, another instructor grabs my right upper arm and holds on. The platform is small with a wood railing on the three sides not facing the pool. He keeps looking down as if waiting for clearance. I keep looking at the horizon beyond the rigging building.

The tanned instructor says, "Don't forget what the sergeant said. Push out away from the platform and then feet first. Push up to the surface, hit the quick release on the harness, strip it off your shoulders, and pull the cord on the floatation jacket. Okay?"

I nod my head up and down. The instructor raises his right fist straight up in the air, and then, with his left, which is still holding on to my arm, he gives me a firm push. I look down at the platform to find the edge. With my boots on the edge, I quickly look up at the roof of the rigging building. I don't look down. I take a deep breath and push off.

I keep looking at the roof until I feel my boots hit the water. I don't even remember falling through the air. I'm under, and I flap my arms and kick my boots frantically while I'm still falling down through the water. My eyes snap open, and I see that the water is a light green. I don't know how far below the surface I am, but I keep moving my arms and legs because I don't want to go any deeper than I already am. The water looks a little lighter green over my head, and I dog-paddle toward the lighter green. My boots feel heavy and I can hardly kick. I keep pushing down on the water. Where is the top? Going to need some air pretty soon. I keep grabbing water and pushing down. I can see something big and yellow over my head. A couple of more pushes and my head is out of the water!

I gasp for air and dog-paddle to remain on top. I push the quick-release button on the parachute harness my chest. Nothing happens. I slam down on the button with my fist and the shoulder straps come loose. The straps fall away from my shoulders, and I catch them and push them down and away. I feel around the bottom edge of the yellow Mae West for the air-release cord, and then I'm flailing my arms as hard as I can just to keep my face out of the water. Finally I find the cord with the wooden ball at the end and yank down. I can hear the inflation but I'm still getting no help keeping my face out of the water. I find the other ball and pull down, and the vest continues to grow. I'm floating, and then the top of the vest climbs tight under my chin and forces my face upward. I'm looking at the sky and it's okay with me, because my face is out of the water. My arms hang loose and I take deep breaths. The water keeps rising and falling on my face. I paddle to turn in a circle and find that the yellow raft is only five feet away to my left. I try to turn on my back but the flotation jacket keeps me from getting on my back so I paddle to the raft. My head hits the raft and I look up. The damn thing is bobbing near my face but I see nothing to grab onto. My face is a few inches above the water but the damn raft is at least eighteen inches high. Shit. The sergeant said the raft would be upside down, and I guess it is, but from where I am, I can't tell. I paddle to stay near the raft and wait a minute until my breathing slows down.

With my arms stretched up onto the top, I pull myself to climb on. I pull up six inches and fall back. The sergeant had said there was a rope attached to the bottom side of the raft to turn it over. I move to the middle of the raft, looking and feeling for a rope. *Got it!* I hold on to the rope while my gasping breaths settle. I have the rope in my hand but can't see it. I lunge up and grip the rope with my other hand. Need to get on top and figure how to turn it over. I pull hand over hand, but I'm not getting any higher on the raft. *Damn it!* Then I can see a little bit of the far side of the raft. Yellow. I pull again. I wasn't moving up but the far side of the raft was riding a little higher! Wasn't getting on top but the raft was turning up and over! Hand over hand. Raft almost vertical. Another tug and the raft is falling on my head. That's okay with me. *A yellow raft on my head is just fine.* After I push myself out from under the raft, I see fabric handles. I lunge for one and hang on. I find another handle and boost myself up. My chest is on the raft, but my legs are still in the water. The Mae West is in my way. I turn on my side, and on the third try, I get one boot onto the raft. I stop for air. Pulling on both handles and sliding my leg, I jerk myself up and over the edge, then finally slide into the raft and just lie there on my face. After a couple of minutes, I roll onto my back and look at the sky. Soon, the raft is moving, being pulled to the edge of the pool. And then I see who is dragging me in.

"Good job," the guy in the trunks says as he pulls on the rope attached to the front of the raft. "Took you only a few minutes to turn that raft over. You done this before?"

TURNING THE RAFT

I shake my head no. "Feels like I was out there for an hour and a half, not a few minutes. It might have seemed like a few minutes to you; your feet were dry."

He smiles. "Just one more thing. The easiest way to get out of the pool and get up here on the deck is to roll back into the water and climb up the ladder at the end of the pool."

I struggle to get up on my knees, noting that the ladder is ten feet away. I fall face-first into the pool. The Mae West bounces hard up against my chin as I paddle to the ladder. When I have climbed halfway up the ladder, I hear a loud splash as the next man's boots hit the water. The instructor has already turned the raft upside down and is pulling it toward the platform end of the pool.

"Enough," I said, as I stand at the top of the ladder.

Could I do that in the dark? Jump out of a sinking, ditched aircraft or get free of a parachute when it hits the water? When I release the chute, will it and the shroud lines come down on me? Could I find the raft and turn it over in a choppy sea?

Chapter Six

A Walk in the Woods

Up the ladder and into a C-47 that looks older than I am … Inside, canvas seats line both sides of the plane. I add my flight bag to the pile at the rear of the cabin and sit close to the front. Uniform for this air ride is flight suit, boots, cap, and dog tags. I look at the passengers around me. I don't know any of them, and it looks like we are about twenty men, all wearing sullen morning faces, not quite ready for the day. We are the chosen few, selected from all three squadrons of the 6th Bomb Wing, deemed in need of Summer Survival training.

I would like to sleep but the web canvas seat must have been designed for maximum discomfort. I'm not too happy, but I don't think anyone gives a damn about how happy I am.

We taxi for just a few minutes, turn onto a runway, and after a short takeoff roll, we lift into the air. I guess the takeoff roll seems short to me because what I'm used to is the forever roll of a B-36 before it lifts off. We're flying to Stead Air Force Base, Nevada, home of the SAC crew Survival Training School. The school is located on the high desert, at an altitude of 5,026 feet at the foot of the Sierra Nevada Mountains. The mountains are heavily forested, steep, and ideal for providing punishment in both summer and winter seasons.

We arrive at Stead, have lunch, and late that same afternoon have a four-hour class on setting animal traps, use of parachute material, starting a smokeless fire, and first aid. I genuinely would rather be some other place, maybe any other place.

Our mission, after being dropped off, will be to reach a designated pickup location forty miles northwest of the drop-off point. Two instructors will accompany our leaderless group, observing, taking notes, and allowing us to get lost if that be the case. I don't feel that they will be offering much help unless life or death is in the balance, and I'm not even sure that would be enough motivation for them to intervene.

And then the instructor launches into the hypothetical tale we're about to become a part of. We are told that we are flying at 20,000 feet altitude. We have completed a successful combat flight mission and know that we do not have enough fuel to take us home. It is actually a scenario most crew members expect if we are ever ordered to make a drop on the USSR and we are lucky enough to survive the blast. As the story goes, we parachute from our B-36 over hostile territory. The flight crew is expected to survive, evade capture, and hike to a designated location for extraction. The rescue aircraft will be a C-47 equipped with rocket booster engines that will require very little runway for takeoff. I roll my eyes in disbelief. Most B-36 crew members believe that this is a fairy tale, but a fairy tale is better than nothing at all. We are told that if we are captured on this exercise, the crew members will be held for an indefinite period of time at a prisoner of war camp. If interned in a POW camp, then we are make every effort to escape.

The time is 1515 hours on Monday, 16 August 1954. It's a nice day. Flight suit, underwear, socks, boots, cap, and dog tags make up the mission uniform. In addition to all that, I am carrying a pad and ballpoint pen in a zippered pocket. I'm ready. Our transportation consists of two Air Force-type trucks. I climb aboard and ease myself onto a side bench in the bed of the first canvas-covered truck. Ten crewmen and one instructor board each truck. Our instructor is easy to spot. He is wearing fatigues and an orange cap, has a backpack, and is holding a walking stick. We are mostly silent as we head into the mountains and the loud truck engine noise fills the air.

The instructor, sitting at the front of the truck bed, tells us, "My name is Tech Sergeant Huskins. I will be with you on this walk in the woods, as will another instructor who is already on site. Our job is only to observe, so you might just as well forget that we're with you. One topo map has been issued to the highest-ranking crew member in your group, with the drop-off point identified and also the location of the extraction point. As you already know, pickup will be by a C-47 modified for short takeoff capability, at 0700 six days from today. Any questions?"

No one says anything.

"None? Okay. At the back of the truck, under the benches are eleven #10 cans, one for each of us. We have, for your convenience, attached a wire handle to each can, along with a foil cover. Each can contains fresh food and ice to keep it cool.

"After we ride for a while, the truck will slow down, and on my signal, those at the rear will grab a can and exit the moving truck. All will follow and I will be last. We will have with us two used parachutes that you have recovered after your crew jumps from your aircraft."

When it is my turn, I pick up a can and jump out of the back of the slow-moving truck. One of our crew is standing on the road holding a paper over his head, not far from another instructor. As we gather around him, I notice that all the trees on both sides of the road are growing tight up against one another and crowd right up to the road.

The crewman is still holding the map over his head.

"I am Major Al Johnson, second pilot in the 24th Squadron," he calls out. "Anyone here outrank me?"

Silence. The two parachutes are on the ground at his feet. Our two instructors stand silently a short distance away.

"Okay," Major Johnson says. "It will be dark soon and we need to set up a one-night camp, get organized, and be up and out of here early morning. Right now, we will walk on this road until we find some kind of a clearing. Men closest to the chutes pick them up and bring them along. Do we have any captains in our group?"

One man raises his hand: "Captain Stark, engineer out of the 39th Squadron."

"Good. Captain, please join me and we'll walk and talk," the major says.

Then he sets a lively pace up the road. We all follow.

Half an hour later, we find a small clearing at the side of the road.

Captain Stark calls out, "Gather round. We will use this clearing. Need to make up two shelters from the chutes and one fire. If we need more space for the shelters, use the road. We sure don't expect much traffic on the road tonight. The cans are half full of food. I imagine you have already looked. We will be on our own for six days, so ration that food for yourself so that it will last you six days. Cook the raw beef tonight or as soon as possible since it won't last long if it's raw."

Major Johnson then takes over: "Country boys, hunters, and Boy Scouts, do what you know needs to be done. City slickers, watch, help, and learn. On this hike, getting to the pickup point is priority number one. There is no priority number two."

A flurry of activity begins. A fire soon crackles, and two parachute shelters take shape, with cut shroud lines tied to tree limbs to support the tops of the shelters and rocks holding the perimeters down. A shallow latrine trench is scraped out of the soil a short distance away, under the trees, and some optimists make and set out small-animal snare traps. Each man gathers leaves and small branches to cover some ground in his tent to sleep on.

The #10 cans each hold a chunk of beef, three small carrots, and four small potatoes in cold water. Most of us place our cans on the fire and make a stew of sorts. The fire provides little light, and darkness forces most of the men to turn in as soon as it gets dark. I can hear night sounds from the woods as I try to sleep.

Early the next morning, as soon as it's light, we carefully take down the shelters. Everything is saved and packed to move. Finally, we bury the remains of the dead fire.

Major Johnson calls us together. "I am passing around the one map we have, showing our drop-off point and pickup location. You will see that we need to travel northwest about three hundred thirty-five degrees and a distance of forty miles if it were straight-line travel. We all know that our walk will not be straight-line travel, so we will cover as much ground as possible each day. At 0700 hours on day number six, we will be picked up by a C-47 modified with two jet packs to allow short runway takeoff. We will need to prepare a clearing for the C-47. Questions?"

"Additional water and food?" asks someone in the group.

"As we find and make use of on the way," is the major's response.

"Will the instructors help with directions?"

"As far as we are concerned, the instructors are out of sight and out of mind. Let's go."

Our crew is lead by Major Johnson, accompanied by a staff sergeant. Captain Stark is our safety man, last in line. I look down at the boots of the man in front of me and start a steady, mindless walk through the woods.

Johnson said forty miles as the crow flies. But we'll be walking through valleys, up and down small hills, and around big hills. The way we need to go, we'll be walking a hundred miles—a hell of a lot more than forty.

Major Johnson sets up a pattern. We walk for fifty minutes and then rest for ten.

Glad that I don't need to carry much else except this miserable covered can and, of course, a parachute for an hour at a time whenever my turn comes up.

A fist is raised at the front of our single-line column and most of us pick a tree to lean against, while some of the men sit on the dead leaves covering the ground.

* * * * *

"Today is the third day," the man behind me says to no one in particular. "Think we're halfway there?"

"Must be," I reply. "Major says we're doing fine."

Man in front says, "At least we've found plenty of water in the valleys. Personally, I'm glad some guys know how to catch fish with a bent wire hook and some shroud line—and even more, that they know how to clean them."

My beef is gone but my can is now carrying some kind of fish and potato soup. A tech sergeant caught, skinned, and boiled a porcupine that he trapped yesterday. The men who added a chunk of the porcupine to their can of soup say it tastes like a mouth full of pine needles, but I didn't see anyone throw it away.

My feet and legs are sore, but no blisters so far. Seems like we are always walking uphill. *When do we find some downhill? Feel sorry for the forty-year-olds. Must be tougher when you are old.* The master sergeant doesn't look so good, but doesn't fall behind, either. Every time we stop for ten minutes, I think he falls asleep, but he is ready when the rest of us are.

77

The sky is clear, the sun is bright, and the air temperature would be just right—*if I didn't have to walk uphill all the time.* Yesterday, when we stopped by a stream for lunch, I stripped and stood in the water and rubbed water on my face and in my armpits and crotch. The water was cold ... very cold. I felt better even though I had to put back on the same underwear, socks, and flight suit. I still smell pretty bad, but no one around me complains, knowing that he probably doesn't smell any better.

*　*　*　*　*

Winter survival in November of last year was miserable, much worse than this summer hike. I was wearing my insulated jacket and pants over my flight suit, plus a woolen cap, gloves, and fur-lined boot overshoes, and I was cold most of every day except when I was standing real close to a fire. When I jumped from the back of the truck then, holding onto my damn can of food, I landed in twelve inches of snow. On that trip, we had to survive four days in the same location, then walk on the fifth day to a pickup point. Our crew for winter survival was made up of ten men, all from the 40th Squadron, plus two instructors who also observed from a distance. That first day, we had some time before darkness to build a couple of fires, set up tents, and stuff the tents with evergreen branches to sleep on. I remember that our cans of food had to be thawed before we could cook the food.

I was cold all night but still hated to get up and move in the morning. Ground animals left tracks in the snow and we set traps. I made a soup with whatever was in the can and added more water every day and made it last four days. I walked away from camp every day in a different direction looking for anything we could eat or use. Everyone searched, but we never found a stream or fish. Sometimes I was too cold to want to eat. Staying warm was on the top of my list.

On the fifth day, we broke camp and hiked. We took turns carrying the chutes and also took turns at the head of the line to pack down the snow for those following. We rotated into that position for fifty minutes at a time.

The weather had been overcast most of every day. I keep looking at the boots of the man in front of me. I learned to keep a steady pace, my feet moved out in front of me, and I thought about nothing. My food can was empty. But we had only one more night to sleep in our chute tents, one more fire to build, and then one more dinner of hot water.

Next morning, we broke camp for the last time. The uphill slope finally gave way to level land. Our pace picked up a little, so we figured we must be getting close. We could see the pickup point, a fairly flat snow-covered meadow. Time was about 1400 hours. We had been told that the pickup plane would be a C-47 equipped with skis and one jet-assist engine mounted on each wing to allow for a very short takeoff roll. Sounded like someone's pipe dream to me.

At 1600 hours, we were in the trees at the edge of the meadow, just sitting in the snow, exhausted. After about twenty minutes, the two instructors came out of the woods. The red-cheeked instructor, who seemed to be enjoying the entire exercise, said, "Congratulations! Original plans have changed. Instead of a ride in a C-47 on skis, tomorrow we are going to hike about one hour to meet with the two trucks that dropped you off. Again, congratulations."

"Shit," I muttered as I sat on one of the chutes that we had been carrying, and then I closed my eyes. I doubted that anyone had ever seen this C-47 with skis and a jet engine. It was all bullshit.

We did have to make camp one more night. Miserable. We had all run out of food, and I doubted if anyone slept very much. I was dead tired but too cold and pissed off to sleep any longer than twenty minutes at a time.

It all ended very early the next morning. It had started snowing during the night and was still snowing when I woke up and heard movements. Our instructors came forward, told us that snow was expected to continue for three more days. Time to get out. We hiked a couple of miles to the waiting trucks, loaded up, and were hauled back to Stead. I slept all the way back sitting in that canvas seat and felt like a frozen fence post when we got back to base.

* * * * *

I am getting weary of this summer walk in the woods. One day runs into another. I am almost out of food, and sleeping on the ground is getting old. I've lost count of how many days we have been walking. It no longer seems important. Every day is like the day before.

The major, though, lets us know that it is the fifth day, and when we begin walking, I am still looking at the boots of the man in front of me. Just like in winter training, I have learned to keep a steady pace. My feet move out in front of me and I think about nothing. My food can is empty. One more night. One more fire to build, erect the chute tents one more time, and then hot water for dinner.

The man in front of me stops. I stop. I look up and see that everyone in front of me is closing up. The major has his fist up in the air. The men behind me close up. We stand and wait.

Major Johnson yells out, "Just beyond the trees in front of us is the meadow we have been looking for. It is fairly flat and clear of trees. We are almost at the pickup point."

I don't hear anyone cheer, but it is good news. Time is about 1800 hours.

"We will stop now," the Major calls out, "and we will stay here tonight. Captain Stark and one other man will move forward and take a look at the landing area. We will be up at 0500 hours to be ready at the edge of the meadow at 0700. We carry everything out with us. This place needs to look like we were never here."

An instructor walks out from the trail that we had just hiked. He has been walking the same trail and hanging back so that we could not hear or see him.

"Congratulations, gentlemen," he said. "You have met your mission objectives. You have survived, and located and arrived at your pickup point on schedule."

Chapter Seven

POW

"Major Johnson," a loud voice calls from the trees, "your crew is surrounded by a unit of the SSAP—the Survival School Air Police. Each of you stay where you are."

Two lines of men, one on each side of our group, walk out of the trees, wearing woodland camouflage. I'm up on my feet, and then we all just stand there, muttering, cursing, and grunting. The Air Police close in on us and stand in two lines about ten feet away. There must be twenty of them.

Up front, I can see one of the "enemy" approach Major Johnson. He salutes crisply and says, "Sir, my name is Brown, T. E., master sergeant in charge of this SSAP unit. Your crew is captured."

Major Johnson returns the salute and says, "I understand, Master Sergeant Brown."

"Sir, if you and your men will follow me and do as you are told, we will have no problems."

The sergeant turns left and heads into the trees, followed by the major, captain, and then the rest of us in a single file. We are a raggedy-assed bunch—dirty, tired, and hungry. Our heads hang as we carry our damn empty food cans and look down at our boots.

We have been captured.

The Air Police form a line on each side of us, ten feet away. Young faces, each man dressed in forest camouflage, shiny black boots, and new helmets, and each man is carrying a black baton—the enemy.

Fifteen minutes later, we are at a road, where four vehicles are waiting for us—a pickup truck and three stake-beds.

This road was only fifteen minutes from us? We must be playing a game of pin the tail on the donkey ... and I sure feel like the donkey.

The closest vehicle is the pickup truck, painted brown.

"Prisoners will file past the pickup and throw into the bed the parachutes, cans, and anything else in your hands. Then load up the trucks," says the master sergeant in charge.

As we file past the pickup to the stake-bed trucks, with guards on both sides, our hands are pulled behind us, and then plastic cuff straps tie our wrists tightly. The truck has a short ladder welded at the back. I'm pushed up the ladder and shoved onto a truck bed, landing on my knees. I roll and scramble up before the man behind me is pushed up and on top of me. I sit on the bench. These trucks are brown with canvas canopy roofs. Seven prisoners load first, with Air Police filling the remaining space on each truck. Three trucks.

No one says anything. *At least we're not walking,* I think. I'm hungry, thirsty, tired, dirty, and smell bad. I close my eyes, listen to the motor of the truck on the dirt road. Seems like only a few minutes' ride. The truck stops.

"Everybody out."

I climb down. The truck is stopped parallel to a twelve-foot-high fence made up of vertical logs, jammed tight against each other with coiled barbwire on top. We are lined up, with guards on the perimeter eyeing us. The area outside the fence is clear of trees and bushes, and the soil is plowed into neat rows.

A pair of gates in the fence stands open and we are herded in, the guards now using their batons to poke us when we don't move fast enough. The sky is becoming dark and night is closing in.

I'm in a goddamn prison. Thought we were finished with this shit.

The fence encloses a yard that looks to be about a hundred feet square. Metal buildings line one side of the yard, and one building is sitting alone on the opposite side. All the buildings are about fifteen feet away from the fence. At the four corners of the yard stand wood towers, about twenty feet high. The wood towers are flat on top, and on each flat top is a machine gun on a tripod. Two men wearing sidearms are positioned at each machine gun.

At the center of the enclosed area is a group of about forty prisoners, all in flight suits, standing, sitting, or lying on the ground. They're not talking to each other or standing in groups. They are listless and look as if they feel worse than I do.

I'm getting bad vibrations. How long have these people been here? Most look exhausted and are doing nothing more than staring at their own boots. Look like they have been worked over and are surviving as best they can.

Helmeted guards stand at the doors of each building. They walk us close to the fence, and the guards with batons form a line between us and the yard.

Suddenly a speaker system blares: "Welcome to Camp Nine." Then military music, very loud, fills the air. It is so loud that I want to cover my ears, but I can't because my hands are cuffed tight behind my back. The men in the middle of the yard just stare at us. They look sullen and beaten down. They just keep staring at us.

The guards, using their batons, prod each man in our group so that the line moves forward, and then we are lined up in front of one of the metal doors at the first building. The loud, irritating music is making my head pound. I think that's what it is supposed to do, and it's working real well. Floodlights illuminate the entire yard, especially the fencing. Must be cold because I'm shivering.

The door that we are lined up in front of opens from the inside, and the first six men in line are prodded with batons and pushed through the door. The rest of us stand and wait in silence. The guards shut down any conversation in our line with a sharp slap of their batons. Mixed in with the loud music, I can hear yelling, grunts, and screams. *Are the people noises coming from the buildings or through the PA system along with the music just to scare us?* Now I'm third in line.

I'm feeling queasy. *These guys are American military men playing the roles of prison guards, right? They're not going to hurt us.* I'm cold. I turn around to the man behind me, but before I can say anything, I'm quickly rewarded with a sharp and painful baton jab to the ribs. The face of the guard who prodded my ribs glares at me, waiting for an excuse to use the baton again.

We stand and wait for at least a half-hour and then the next six of us are prodded through the door, one at a time. No one has come out of the building through this door.

I stand just inside the door, wondering what is coming next. A deadbolt is pulled, and another door opens ahead of me before I am pushed into a dim corridor. I can see exposed wood studs for walls, and there are metal doors on both sides of the hall.

Dressed in pressed camouflage fatigues, boots, shiny helmet, and carrying a sidearm, a son of a bitch drives a baton into the middle of my back and pushes hard until I move faster along the hall. Halfway down the corridor, he opens a door, puts a hand on my shoulder, and propels me through the opening, where my flight suit is grabbed by two guards. They spin me around and drop me into a metal chair that is bolted to the floor. A belt in thrown across my legs, pulled tight, and then snapped closed.

The room has bright lights, the walls are covered with old, stained, torn padding, and the floor is dirty, stained concrete. The smell of vomit is so strong that I gag … and I have needed to take a piss for a long time. Standing in front of me are two guards with helmets and an older guy who is not wearing a helmet. One of the guards wraps a blindfold around my head, covering my eyes. Black on black.

"Name, rank, and serial number," snaps someone I assume to be the old guy.

I hesitate. My mouth is so dry that I open it then close it, but no answer comes out.

I can feel the old man stick his face close to mine and he bellows, "Name, rank, and serial number!" His breath is foul and spittle sprays onto my face.

"Hall, William L., Lieutenant, AO3024003!" I yell out.

"What the fuck is your rank, asshole? First or second lieutenant?"

"First," I grunt.

Nothing has happened to me yet and my face is sweaty and I need to pee real bad. Somebody cuts the cuffs from my wrists.

These guys are US military, aren't they?

"What's your job on the crew?"

I don't say anything. Somebody hits me hard on the side of the head with a padded board.

In my face, but softly now: "I just want to know what job you had on the plane while you were dropping bombs on my family."

"Hall, William L., First Lieutenant …"

I can hear movement behind me. Somebody slaps me on the side of my head again, but harder, with the same board.

"I need to hear this shit talk to me. I ain't got all day."

What feels like a length of wire is wrapped around each wrist and then laced between my fingers. No sound at all—except I can hear a humming noise start up behind me.

"Ugh," I crow. "What the fuck are you doing?"

No response.

The humming noise grows louder.

What the hell is that? Turning on a machine? Someone must have thrown a switch … and here I am with wires wrapped around my hands. Great …

A jolt of pain shoots through both my hands and arms, and I stifle a groan. I try to shake off the wires from around my hands, but while I'm trying to get them off, another rack of pain, stronger than the first, shoots through my hands and arms. Both my arms jump up in the air like a protest against the burning in me. I scrape at my hands, trying to get rid of the wires, but another jolt reaches me before I can. Finally, the wires come off. I slump in the chair, exhausted but glad to be free of the wires and the pain.

"Now, what was your job?"

"I'm in charge of the gunners!" I yell. "I fly in the back of the plane. I didn't drop any bombs!"

"A first lieutenant gunner. Bullshit."

I feel like throwing up. *That was a stupid answer.*

"I don't even know what they do up front," I say.

"Take this shit out of here."

I'm hit across the thighs with a baton, and the belt is loosened. Hands pull up on the front of my flight suit and I'm on my feet—but the blindfold is still on my face. I'm pulled out the door and down the corridor. I don't feel so good. I'm pushed through another door that I just heard creak open. The blindfold is pulled off and I am pushed through the doorway and hear a lock slam home.

Some light from outside comes through a foot-square hole in the wall near the ceiling. The floor is concrete and the walls are of concrete block. The room is about six feet by eight feet and is around seven feet high. A metal bucket sits in the corner on the floor. I piss into the bucket and then I lie on my side on the concrete floor, my arms wrapped around my shoulders. I'm cold. *Glad they stopped with the fucking electricity, at least.*

This room is too small and I feel a terror start to build up in me. I sit up on the floor and I close my eyes. I'm at the top of a hill at the ski area in Bend, Oregon. My best mental escape. The sun is shining, my face is cool. I slide off the ski lift and stand at the top of Dogleg Run. I can see the lodge at the bottom of the hill, three chair lifts moving up the hill, skiers wearing bright red and blue jackets on the slopes, and a crowd close to the lodge. I breathe long, deep breaths. I am satisfied to just stand and look down the slope. The terror is still close, though. I feel better with my eyes closed.

I hear the thunk of a lock and the door opens. Had I fallen asleep? A guy wearing a helmet and camo fatigues comes in carrying two slices of brown bread in a plastic bag and a metal bowl and spoon. He sets them on the floor just inside the door. The metal door slams shut again. I crawl to the bowl and look at it. The stew, the bowl, and spoon look clean enough.

Guess they don't want us to get sick and vomit all over their floor.

I sit on the floor with my back against a wall. The soup is warm, with carrots, potatoes, and brown meat. The bread is old and stale.

They're feeding me, so I guess they don't want us to keel over, either.

Before I can finish the soup, the door opens again.

"Get your ass up and out!" says the mouth below the helmet at the door.

I grab the bread and shove it into my pocket, and slowly push up from the floor. The cell is getting dark now. *Is this guy seven feet tall or is it just the helmet?* He cuffs my hands in front of me, not behind my back. As I walk through the door, he holds my arm just below the shoulder and steers me toward another metal door at the end of the corridor.

One of the doors along the hall is open. The guard slows down at the open door and shoves me into the room so I can have a look. The room is empty except for two round wooden covers on the floor. The covers have a two-inch hole in the center of each. One cover has two fingers sticking out from below through the hole, and the other hole shows no fingers.

"Want to see?" the guard says.

With his boot, he kicks aside the cover without fingers. I see a man standing in a pit full of water, up to his chin. The water is dark brown. With the cover on the pit, it would leave about six inches from the top of the water to the underside of the cover. The man's back is toward us. His head is back, his face up, his eyes closed, and I can see in the dirty water that his hands are cuffed in front of him. He moans.

Then, from the other pit, the one with two fingers sticking out of the hole in the cover, I hear someone scream, "I hear you, you cock-sucking son of a bitch. Let me out of here, you bastard. I can't breathe." Then, after a moment, quiet and pleading: "Please let me out."

The two fingers disappear from the hole. I stare.

I feel like I'm going to vomit. My heart is racing. *They can't do that! This is crazy.* My legs feel weak.

The hand in my armpit pulls me back out of the room.

"The one doing the yelling," the guard says as he pushes me along into the corridor, "he punched a guard in the face."

I say nothing. My throat is dry and my eyes watery. I am worried that I might end up in a hole. I'm definitely not punching anybody.

Before we reach the end of the hall, the guard puts a black cloth bag over my head and pushes me into a room. He cinches the bag snug and I panic, pulling away from him. *I can't breathe!*

"Jesus!" I yell.

There is a hole in the bag near my mouth. The guard shoves me down onto the floor. I can hear the door lock. I'm breathing short, fast breaths. I get up on my knees with my face down, and the fabric of bag falls away from my face. I'm breathing air from the hole in the bag. No light comes through the hole. The room must be dark. My hands are cuffed in front of me. I pull the bag up and away from my face. All I can hear is my own breathing. I stay on my knees and I'm still breathing. Not dead yet. My breathing slows down and I can't hear anything else. I feel lost. The room is absolutely black. Not a sliver of light. I get up on one knee, then up on my feet. I take some small steps forward with my cuffed hands out in front of me. I hit a wall … and can feel that it is covered with padding. I turn my shoulder to feel the wall, and with my shoulder against the wall, I take small steps along the wall. Four corners and a door. Finally, I sit with my back against a wall.

"Hello," I say. "Anybody hear me?"

The sound is absorbed and I can barely hear myself.

"Yahhhhhh!" I yell.

I can think of … nothing.

No light, no sound. Isolation. My eyes burn and I close my eyes on the burning.

I lie on the floor and think. I need to take my mind back to the ski slope again, but I can't hold the picture and my mind keeps slipping back into the silent room. *Up on the ski slope. Up on the ski slope.*

Time passes. I don't know how long. The door opens and dim light from the hallway silhouettes a man in the doorway. I can hear footsteps … soft footsteps. I can see the broad back of the guard as he turns around and walks out. The door closes behind him and lights are turned on. Bright lights, all in the ceiling. The lights are turned up brighter, aimed down toward all the walls and reflected off the wall material. No matter where I look, my eyes hurt. The lights are bright through my eyelids even when I keep my eyes closed. Then the noise comes on, so loud it hurt my ears. Maybe it's military music, very loud with shrieks, banging, whistles, drums, and rumbling all mixed in. The sound is beating on my ears and filling my head so I can think of nothing but the noises and the beating drums.

I lie on the floor. My hands are still cuffed. The light comes through my closed eyes, the noise fills my body. I can think no thoughts. Skiing? Can't.

I curl up on the floor, with my knees drawn up to my chest. Nothing stops. On and on for a long time. Noise and lights. Noise and lights. Drums, shrill whistles, and rumbling loud music.

The lights are turned off, and the room is now colored black. The sound stops. Silence. The sound has stopped, yes, but I still hear it in my head. Finally, even that noise stops. It finally stops. I didn't realize how tight and strained my body was until I start to relax. My muscles hurt all over my body.

Is it only three minutes later? My body jumps and twists as the noise and brightness return full blast. Fetal position like a reflex. With my eyes closed, the sound seems louder than before.

Does it last four minutes? Everything stops. I'm in the fetal position again. *When will it start again?* I can't think and I'm taking short shallow breaths.

Every muscle is tight and tensed, and I don't know how long I lie that way. Three minutes? Five minutes? How many starts and stops? I don't know. I don't much care anymore. The door opens and I lie still. Hands under both arms lift me to my feet. I stand but do not move, my eyes still closed. With my eyes shut, two men move me through the door and along the corridor. Through another door and into a another room. I open my eyes.

The room is big, with windows, tables, and chairs. There is a filled pitcher and glasses on the tables. Wrapped sandwiches fill a tray. Six men dressed in flight suits either sit on chairs or on the floor with their backs against a wall, or lie on the floor with their eyes closed. No one speaks and no one eats. We are drained.

A guard is in the room. He is dressed in cameo but wears no helmet and does not carry a baton. He circulates in the room quietly, asking those who have been in the room for a while if they are ready to move on. Two say yes, one shakes his head no. The two that say that they are ready to move on slowly follow the guard out a door. Time passes. Crewmen leave; others come in from the corridor.

I drink a glass of orange juice. I have a headache and I'm pissed off ... and I want to sleep. After a while, a guard says something to me that I barely hear or understand. I follow him through yet another door and then outside into the yard. The sky is dark and the lights in the yard are lit. Air is cool and feels good. I lie on the ground on my back and my mind rambles.

I guess we got just a taste of a POW camp. Realistic enough for me. In that room with the noise and lights, I forgot for a while that this was all make-believe. I really don't want to do that again.

If we ever had to fly our combat mission, would we even get to the target? Setting aside all the mechanical things that could go wrong, we would fly our preplanned route. Interceptors are improving every month and could reach us at 40,000 feet. Right now they cannot. But next month? We reach the fuckin' target, drop, and run. Would our escape maneuver allow the aircraft to survive the fury of our own bomb? No one really knows. We are supposed to land at a recovery field if the USSR hasn't obliterated it already. Running out of fuel from a damaged aircraft, we bail out. I don't think the B–36 would do well ditching or crash landing. Parachute into enemy territory? We would be killed by any local with a pitchfork who would know that we had just dropped a bomb on their people. Evade and survive? Do I believe a C–47 would pick us up someplace? Strictly a pipe dream. Would any crew member make it to a POW camp and then survive the camp? Are you kidding? If we ever made it back home, would there be a "back home" left when we got there? I don't think so, and it's good that this is the only time I'm ever going to think about it.

The sky looks lighter. I can hear loud static from the PA system.

"Congratulations, gentlemen. You have completed your introduction to POW Camp Number Nine. My name is Kelson, Lieutenant Colonel, US Air Force, in charge of this facility and its operation. A few comments and then you will be transported back to Stead Air Force Base. The electric shocks you have experienced have been small. Our research tells us that prisoners in Korea were routinely subjected to voltages that knocked them out of their chairs, rendering them unconscious or even bringing on strokes. Interrogation, the isolation cell, silence, and noise would routinely be applied for hours, days, or weeks. The enemy will break you if they want to and if they have enough time. Chemicals and drugs are the most effective, but the damage they cause is almost always irreversible.

"The two men in the water-filled pits are part of our staff, not prisoners. We take turns. Your guards have been officers or enlisted men ranked tech sergeant or higher of the Survival School Air Police, US Air Force. They have all received special training before being assigned to this duty, and have gone through the same treatment as each of you prisoners … twice. Again, congratulations to you crew members of B–36 aircraft, Strategic Air Command. Please exit through the gates where transportation to Stead is standing by.

Article from Reno Gazette-Journal appearing in November 1955

Training Story Brings Question From Pentagon

Sept 7th 1955

Stead Commander Called to Capitol As Article Published

Col. Burton E. McKenzie, commander of Stead Air Force base was enroute to Washington today for questioning about a story appearing in Newsweek magazine concerning highly realistic measures of physical and mental pressure, borrowed from the Communists, being used at Stead to train Air Force crewmen to resist brainwashing.

The magazine in its current issue describes an unusual 17-day course being given at Stead where it said the air crews undergo hunger, pain, fatigue and mental pressure to teach them to survive in enemy territory or captivity.

TELLS OF WASHOUTS

It speaks of "ingenious combinations of physical and mental stresses," and tells of men who are washed out of combat flying because of their reaction.

Col. McKenzie is being accompanied by other officers on his staff.

Officials said in Washington what the Air Force high com-

DECLINE COMMENT

The public information office at Stead today declined comment on the incident pending further clarification from headquarters in Washington. It is known that representatives of Life Magazine and Time Magazine have visited the base in the last few days, presumably to write articles on the training course.

Confinement, hard labor, prolonged interrogations, barefoot "death marches," spotlights in the face, electric shocks and other devices are used, the report said, in preparing men to face the enemy.

"But the pressures are turned on under supervision of medical men and five psychologists and some 29,000 men have safely withstood the 17-day course," the magazine said in its Pentagon-cleared report.

"Each man is tackled where he is most vulnerable," the story said. "Officers who ask for water get it thrown in the face. Meek 'prisoners' are bounced against the wall by the brawniest interrogator . . . men who are shy about undressing may not keep their shorts on. Interrogators munch

(Turn to page 24, col. 1)

Training Story Brings Question

(Continued from page 1)

sandwiches in front of the hungriest trainees."

The story describes trainees "who blow up violently" and attack "guards" (instructors) others who fall to the ground weeping, or tumble out of box-like confinement" like footballs, their muscles temporarily paralyzed."

At a stockade, where conditions of an enemy POW camp are simulated, trainees break rocks, sleep on the ground without blankets in near-freezing nights, eat "uncooked spinach and raw spaghetti," the account says.

A 36-hour interrogation phase is reported "harmless, but often frightening," electric shocks are used on trainees, along with these other devices:

"'The hole,' 10 feet under ground where men spend hours in darkness, shoulder deep in water; the giant 'coffin' which imprisons trainees flat on its gravel bottom; and the steel 'sweat box' . . ."

The magazine said the course "could not and would not duplicate tortures of Communist captivity," but "methods are adapted from reports of Korean war prisoners and could hardly be more realistic . . .

"To break resistance interrogators try almost anything to

91

Chapter Eight

Briefing for Guam

On the squadron bulletin board:

> 28 August 1954
> 40th Bomb Squadron Deployment
> Staff at 6th Bomb Wing has scheduled aircraft of the 40th Squadron to depart Walker AFB starting 13 Sept 1954 for Anderson Air Force in Guam. Squadron Operations will provide the following to all Aircraft Commanders:
> — Identification of aircraft assigned
> — Date and time of departure
> — Name, rank, and station of each crew member
> — Additional information as required
>
> T. S. Nagel, Colonel
> 40th Bomb Squadron

I guess Squadron Operations can't squeeze in any more training sessions. They are running out of time. The Flight Line Building is hectic with activity. Meetings in the Briefing Room, stacks of papers on most of the desks, and everyone is in a hurry.

"How was survival? Lots of fun, huh?" comes at me from behind my back.

"Yeah, yeah. A walk in the woods," I respond. "Have you been through it yet?"

"No. Scheduled for winter session in February. I hear the skiing is great. When did you get back from Stead?"

"Day before yesterday," I said. "The squadron gave us a day off because we still smelled too bad to be allowed to mingle."

The scheduling board, I find, is filled. *Damn it! They sneaked in one more class.* The squadron managed to work in a LORAN refresher for tomorrow for all navigators and observers. Probably a good idea. *Don't use LORAN very often, but maybe it will help over the big blue Pacific.*

The board shows another notice that reads that everyone in the 40th Squadron needs to report to Wing Personnel sometime today to review personal documents. For me, lunch at the O Club and then to Personnel.

Looks as if the entire squadron is trying to get into the Personnel Office at the same time. Inside, it's not as bad as it looks from the outside. There is a short line and at least twenty men sitting in classroom armchairs all reviewing their files.

I reach the head of the line and I am handed a folder with my name on it, so I sit and look over my papers. Date on papers say that I last reviewed them about two years ago, when I was in Cadet Training. I knew then, as a cadet, that these papers were routine and really didn't apply to me, but I had scanned them and signed them anyway.

Today, I look a little closer. In case of emergency, notify whom? Who is your beneficiary in case you die, and who gets the $10,000 military life insurance payout? What do you want done with your remains? Disability? Power of attorney? Religious preference? Burial instructions? All questions that I don't even want to think about, much less provide an answer to. Burial will be paid for by the US Government, the papers tell me. All of the information is a little more sobering than two years ago. I make no changes, sign the forms, return the file to the counter, and get out of the building.

Next morning, at the Link Trainer Building where LORAN classes are held, the classroom fills, and at 0830 hours, Lieutenant

Colonel Colby walks in. We all rise. Colonel Colby, Select Crew navigator from the 39th Squadron, reviewed celestial for us awhile ago, and today he will review LORAN. He motions us to sit.

"Good morning, gentlemen," Colby says. "We will devote this morning to the review of how to navigate the seas using LORAN. Those of you who have had the pleasure of navigating over the cold Atlantic waters to Thule Air Base in Greenland or over the Pacific to Alaska or northern Japan have made use of, or have tried to make use of, the long-range navigation system. It utilizes radio range signals that, when received by an aircraft or ship at sea, provide the geographical location of the receiver."

"You have all been exposed in navigation school as to how the LORAN system works, so this is a review in case you were asleep at the time. The radio signals are generated by fixed land-based radio beacons. One string of beacon towers is located around the perimeter of the North Pacific Ocean, and a second around the perimeter of the North Atlantic Ocean.

"The beacon towers, one primary and two secondary at each location, provide radio signals precisely time-delayed. These signals are received by LORAN units on ships at sea or aircraft in flight. When signals from two sets of beacon towers are received and properly interpreted, they provide information so that two curved lines can be plotted on your chart. The intersection of these two lines give a geographic location of the LORAN receiver, and therefore a time-dated fix.

"You have all previously been instructed in the use of the LORAN system and you have also been made aware of the limitations of the system.

"The use of LORAN is limited geographically to the North Atlantic and North Pacific because beacon towers are located only in those areas. The radio transmissions are severely affected by weather and many other sources of interference. Reading and interpreting the signals at the receiver can be difficult.

"Your deployment to Guam is to the south, out of beacon coverage. Nevertheless, while in Guam, you might receive orders to fly to a forward base in northern Japan or Alaska. Make the LORAN system work for you. If you find yourself in a situation flying with solid cloud cover above and below, LORAN might just provide you with a fix when you really need one and nothing else is available.

"We are distributing to each of you, copies of signals as you might see them on your LORAN receiver. Read and study them, and ask questions. I will be in the classroom for three hour to assist. Three hours from now, class is dismissed. I personally believe that the LORAN system will soon be replaced by a new navigation system that will be more useful and reliable. Until then, make the most of what you have."

I hope I'm never in the situation where LORAN is all I have. I need to hustle over to the Base Hospital to get my shots. Not scheduled for a physical. Maybe get a chance to talk with a pretty nurse for a few minutes, or more likely an ugly corpsman. Whatever.

Yesterday, all radio operators of the 40th Squadron attended a briefing and received detailed information for the flight to Anderson. Master Sergeant Snell, our primary radio operator, told me he now has information for the flight itself, including all possible alternates and emergencies.

Snell said, "I even have the information I would need if we had to combat-strike from Anderson to targets. My head is going to explode."

* * * * *

In the Flight Line Building, all navigators, observers, and radar personnel of the 40th are being briefed by Lieutenant Colonel Colby. Time is 0830 hours and it is eleven days before our departure date. Projected on an enormous screen behind Colby is a chart showing Walker in the upper-right corner and Guam in the lower-left.

"Good morning, gentlemen," Colby says. "This briefing is to give you an overall picture of our flights to Anderson Air Force Base on Guam. Aircraft of the 6th Bomb Wing will be deployed on the twelfth, thirteenth, and fourteenth of September. Anderson is designated not only as a weapon station but also a forward airfield for the 6th Bomb Wing.

"Long-range weather forecast for the period of time that the 40th Squadron will have aircraft aloft is for scattered or broken cloud cover above our flight altitudes most of the way and 75-percent cloud cover at levels below our flight altitude. A detailed forecast will be provided at flight times.

"The island of Guam has an air-security perimeter in place. Your aircraft commander will call in the information you provide to him for time and location of a penetration of the radar-protected perimeter. Actual penetration needs to be damn close to your estimate or your AC will suffer the embarrassment of his B-36 being met and escorted by two interceptor aircraft with smiling pilots at the controls. Any questions at this time? No? Then Major Lin will continue the briefing."

Major Lin stands at the chart. "I work at Wing Headquarters and am involved in planning of long-distance flights. For security purposes, we have plotted five different routes from Walker to Anderson. The dates of our flights have already been established. Squadron Operations will assign one of the specific flight paths and takeoff times to each aircraft from information provided by Wing."

Lin refers to the map, and then points out and names various islands and rocks in the Pacific Ocean between the West Coast and the Marianas.

"As you can see, once we leave the West Coast, we will not have much available for map-reading and we will be too far south for LORAN. Any questions you may have are to be directed to your Squadron Operations Office. This concludes the briefing. All radar officers, navigators, and observers will meet at your Squadron Briefing Rooms at 1100 hours today for additional information."

At the 1100 hour briefing, I receive a copy of a chart, reduced in size but clear enough to pull the information I need. It plots the flight path assigned to Major Kingby's aircraft, with a departure date and time. Obviously, Wing has planned it all and handed it down. I leave the meeting with plenty of work to do.

There is a lot of blue ocean on that chart and those rocks in the water won't be of much help if we get into trouble. Got to do this right.

The next few days are hectic. Aircraft commanders, pilots, and engineers meet for almost one full day, discussing the flights, including their responsibilities to attain and hold minimum fuel consumption. They also discuss alternate landing fields in case of emergency. *Alternate fields? What alternate fields in the South Pacific?* I bet that must have been an interesting discussion.

* * * * *

At Walker, distances from the Squadron Operations Buildings and the maintenance buildings to aircraft parking aprons are long and need to be traveled many times during a normal workweek by aircraft crews and maintenance men. Trucks are rarely available for these kinds of transportation needs. To minimize this problem, the base allows privately owned scooters and motorbikes on the flight line so individuals can travel to and from the aircraft parking apron. The system works well, with all vehicles registered and insured.

Anderson AFB has the same problem as Walker does in terms of getting to parked aircraft, so the lightweight vehicles used at Walker are deployed with us to make them available at Anderson. Tomorrow at 1700 hours, all lightweight vehicles going to Anderson are to be parked at an area near a designated maintenance building, with gas tanks emptied and batteries disconnected. All these vehicles will be tied down on pallets and hoisted into the B-36 bomb bays for the flight to Guam.

Changes in station, separation from the service, and transfers have all provided steady buy-and-sell opportunities to own a lightweight vehicle. The lightweights are well cared for by their owners, are passed down from owner to owner, and seem to run forever.

* * * * *

Three days before the 39th Squadron starts its departures, all aircraft commanders meet at a wing briefing in the morning and another briefing at squadron level in the afternoon.

Two days before departure, each aircraft commander meets with his crew in the morning to bring them up to date, and that afternoon, the crew meets again for flight briefing.

After Major Kingby completes his portion of the afternoon briefing, I outline the flight plan and timing.

"We will depart Walker at 0800 hours on 13 September and will fly over Phoenix, Arizona, about two hours after takeoff. From Phoenix, we fly a short leg to San Diego, California, ETA at 1130 hours, then over water to Honolulu. That leg will be 2,620 miles and estimated at eleven and one-half hours. We then fly from Honolulu to Wake Island, a ten-and-one-half-hour leg. Final leg from Wake Island is six and one-half hours, 1,500 miles to Anderson Air Force Base on Guam. The total distance is 7,150 miles, and we are estimating thirty-two hours in the air. The usual wind pattern at this time of the year is from the west, so we expect light headwinds for the entire flight."

Thirty-two hours in the air is really pushing the limit. I bet that Captain Cruz, our flight engineer, is going to be monitoring our fuel consumption like a hawk. Losing an engine on this flight to Guam would screw up his fuel calculations and give him an instant ulcer. Our bomb bays will be lightly loaded and that will help hold down our fuel consumption.

Major Kingby closes the briefing: "Tomorrow is a free day for all of us to get organized at home. Twelve September is starting date of departure for the 39th and our 40th crew will be at our Flight Line Building to tie off any loose ends that we might find in our own plans. Our full crew will meet at the Flight Line Building at 0630 hours on 13 September, bright eyed and ready to go. Pilots will be at a weather briefing at 0600 hours. Questions?"

Chapter Nine

Walker to Anderson

Our full crew is at the aircraft at 0645 hours on 13 September. Weather looks good. The thunder of B-36 aircraft with takeoff times earlier than ours fills the air at regular intervals. "Just another flight," we tell each other, but everything is checked twice. Little conversation takes place, with the anxiety and excitement reined in tight.

Personnel on the flight deck finally make a normal takeoff at 0758 hours, heavy because we are topped out with as much fuel as we can take, although our bomb bays carry light loads.

"Navigator to Pilot."

"Pilot here."

"Heading to Phoenix two seven five degrees."

"Pilot. I confirm heading two seven five degrees to Phoenix."

I yell to Panetta, "On our flight from here to Phoenix then on to San Diego, it looks like broken or scattered clouds above and below all the way. We should be able to map-read on both legs even as we climb up and over the Rockies. Piece of cake."

We might as well enjoy the map-reading while we can. The only map-reading after San Diego will be at Hawaii and a few rocks in the Pacific … if we can find them. A long, hopefully boring flight. I have to pace myself and sleep whenever I can.

Panetta is laughing. "Hope we don't run short of fuel and have to lose weight by emptying the bomb bays. If we drop the bikes and scooters in the drink, we would be making a lot of unforgiving enemies of the flight and maintenance crews of the 40th Squadron."

"Ever been to San Diego?" I ask.

"Not yet. I hear it has good weather all year round and lots to do and see. Tijuana's just a few miles south."

"Don't drive a car into Mexico at Tijuana. Turn your back for a few minutes after parking and you may never see that vehicle again," I say.

Our aircraft is now flying directly over San Diego and all is well. We make our turn, becoming feet-wet, and head west over the Pacific toward Hawaii. View out of the greenhouse shows nothing but lots and lots of blue water below.

"Panetta, we will shoot the sun as long as possible, even when it's dipping into the Pacific. A reading about every forty minutes between here and Hawaii. More often if we find a wind shift. Not much to do between readings."

Panetta replies, "Understand. A sun reading every forty minutes."

The engines provide a steady drone, loud, comforting, and boring. I lie my head on my arms on the vibrating nav table between sun shots, but I'm unable to sleep.

Didn't have much breakfast. I don't want to have to use that metal can that we call a toilet. Everyone on the crew knows that it's standard procedure that whoever uses the can cleans it out when we land. I never seem to need to urinate very much in flight. The altitude sucks all the water from my system and I'm always more concerned about dehydration.

I eat two pieces of very cold fried chicken from my in-flight lunch, a small plastic container of fruit cocktail, and drink half a bottle of water.

Major Heller is asleep. He seems to be able to fall asleep for short periods of time while still sitting in his chair. He will be awake as we approach Hawaii to take radar fixes on the islands, but he never passes any of that radar information on to me. The theory is that the navigator needs to navigate even if the radar is down and the pilots are unable to receive any signals from directional radio antennas. Over the Pacific, the radar receives no returns and there are no radio antennas.

Panetta's eyes are closed, but he is not asleep.

"Paul, get some sleep," I tell him.

He opens his eyes, nods okay, and finds a place in the radio room to lie down and sleep. I shoot the sun and plot the fixes, and the sun drops lower in the sky. I call in a heading correction to the flight deck and all is pleasantly routine.

I ask Radio to wake up Panetta, and he takes the navigator seat.

"I'm going to get some sleep, otherwise I won't be worth a damn when we get close to Guam. I'm going to use one of the bunks in the aft compartment," I say.

Panetta's eyes widen. "You're going through the tube?"

"Yeah, through the tube."

I pick up my chest-pack chute and move into the radio room.

"How's everything on the flight deck?" I ask Snell.

"All six are turning. No problems."

"Please inform the flight deck that I am rolling to the aft compartment. Then call the gunner in charge back there and let him know that I'm on my way. He needs to watch me through the window in the tube hatch to make sure I don't get hung up halfway there, and then I want him to open the hatch when I get close. Close this forward hatch as soon as I get moving."

The tube is about eighty-five feet long, the length of the bomb bays, and is thirty-six inches in diameter. It is located on the left side of the fuselage between the outer skin of the plane and the bomb bays, and is the only pressurized connection between the forward and aft crew compartments. In the tube is a flat cart about five feet long, on four small wheels that ride on tracks at the bottom of the tube. It provides a way to travel from the front crew compartment to the gunners compartment at the rear of the plane while in flight and the cabins are pressurized.

I make eye contact with Sergeant Snell, and he acknowledges my instructions with a nod of his head. I shimmy onto the sled in the tube head-first on my back and lay my chest chute on my legs. Eight inches above my face is a steel cable secured to the top of the tube and running its full length. I try not to think of how confining the tube feels. I pull on the overhead cable and the cart rolls aft smoothly. The loss of light from the forward end of the tube tells me that Snell has closed the tube door.

Doors at both ends are now closed and latched, and I concentrate on keeping the cart moving. The reason there is a door at each end of the pressured tube is that, if the forward or rear compartment experiences an explosive decompression, the tube will still have pressure. Without any tube doors, if one of the two compartments suddenly loses pressure while someone is using the tube, that crewman would instantly become a flying projectile toward the unpressurized area. A deadly event to be avoided.

What I have now for illumination is a series of incandescent lamps recessed into the top of the tube, spaced about twenty feet apart. They give off very little light. I'd like to close my eyes, but I need to look for the cable overhead in the dim light. I pull on the cable and move through the tube. I keep pulling on the cable and think only of the cable. Seems like a long ride. Finally, someone opens the aft hatch and bright light floods in. I start to breathe again as I reach out to two handholds on the wall above the hatch, and then I pull myself out. The grinning gunner seems to be enjoying the distress that I'm trying to hide.

"Thanks," I mutter. "Please wake me up in one hour."

"One hour," the gunner responds.

I look around the spacious compartment. The engine noise is even louder back here than up front because we are now flying aft of the engines. The compartment moves constantly in a small arc: left, right, left, right, left, right. That is the penalty for traveling so close to the tail of the plane, but I imagine the gunners don't even notice it with the steady vibration even more severe than up forward. One gunner is at the scanner bubble on the left side, and another gunner is at the bubble on the right side, looking forward. The others are in bunks, sleeping or reading. An empty lower bunk is straight ahead of me. I shuffle back, drop my chute on the bottom end of the bunk, and carefully lie down, using my arm as a pillow. My feet end up straddling the chute.

Someone is soon shaking my shoulder.

"One hour, Lieutenant."

Shit.

I say, "Thanks," rub my face, lie there for a minute, then I'm up. With my chute in hand, I walk to the left-side scanner.

"Please call Radio and let him know that I'm on my way. He needs to look for me and open the forward tube hatch when I get close."

I place my chute on the cart, grab the two handholds over the tube door, pull my legs up, and swing my ass into the tube. I squirm my body around until I'm on my back on the cart with my legs on top of the chute. I haven't gone anyplace yet and I'm already breathing hard.

The scanner looks at me and says, "Ready to go?"

"Ready," I respond and then reach for the cable.

I pull on the cable and move forward, and the scanner slowly closes the hatch door, sealing off the light. I'm fully awake now and looking up at the cable. I pull on the cable again and the cart smoothly moves forward. I have to pull on the cable a little harder than on my trip aft, and I realize that the plane's normal flight attitude must be slightly nose-up, so I'm pulling myself uphill. The tube seems even longer than during my ride aft. My sled hits the stops at the front hatch. By lifting my head, I can see part of the forward hatch. Sergeant Snell is standing there, holding the tube hatch open and waiting for me. I kick my chute out the hatch and slide forward into the radio room. I sure as hell feel relieved to get out of the tube, and I just stand near the tube door for a couple of minutes. After a few minutes, I step down into the lower deck. Panetta is just coming down the ladder from the dome.

"Stars barely visible," he says. "I found just a few constellations still visible and only two target stars, so we will have only a two-star fix.

"Good man," I say and then sit on the floor of the radar compartment.

Panetta plots and then I sit in the nav seat.

"Get some sleep," I say. "I'll shoot and plot."

Later, as I pass Radio, I ask, "Anything new from the flight deck?"

"Number two engine is shut down. The engineer is running all kinds of calculations. Where are we?"

"Hawaii in a couple of hours," I assure him.

Everyone on the crew is flying blind except Panetta and myself. I sure don't like that we have lost an engine already and are still short of Hawaii. Our engineer must have a very large stress headache.

* * * * *

After a while, through the greenhouse I can see the lights of Honolulu off to the right. I wait seven minutes until we intercept our planned course coming out of Hawaii and then call the flight deck with a new heading for Wake Island. I step into the radio compartment and tap Snell on the shoulder so he can come up front to the greenhouse and see the lights of Honolulu as we turn onto our new heading.

Some more chicken from my second boxed meal, and a container of sliced peaches. Panetta wakes up. Hope I look better than he does. We alternate shooting celestial and plotting for what seems a long time. I am tired and bored numb but grateful for an uneventful flight so far. Number two engine has been shut down, which is still a little unsettling, but I can't do anything about it except hope that the engineer has the problem under control. I don't want to think of what a shutdown engine does to his fuel-consumption calculations.

The sun is rising directly behind us now, and the yellow rays reflect off the water. The sky has broken clouds above and a solid cloud deck below. The solid cloud layer below keeps any rock islands hidden from us even if we fly directly over them. Radar should be checking them out.

* * * * *

Wake Island is one of three coral islands that make up the Wake Atoll. The atoll is less than three square miles in area and at its highest elevation is only twenty-five feet above the water. It does have a runway but not much else, and I don't think I would like to spend much time there. Our leg from Hawaii to Wake Island is uneventful. I am pleased that we fly the leg with our five engines still functioning as they should be, and the navigation is routine with winds reasonable and manageable. Everyone is tired and conversation is at a minimum. Boredom is welcome at the right time and place, and the leg between Hawaii and Wake Island is certainly the right time and place. When we fly close enough to Wake, it will show on radar, and it also does have a powerful radio antenna signal. If Radar doesn't find Wake somewhere below us when my navigation says we are over the island, then we have a big problem. I should say that I, as navigator, would have a very big problem. Radar does discover Wake Island where it is supposed to be, and we make a heading change of fifteen degrees to start our last leg to Guam. Flight time will be about seven hours to Anderson.

* * * * *

Guam is a small island in the Mariana chain. It is the most southern and the largest of the group, although it is only eight miles wide and thirty miles long. The island is home to a large naval facility and is a major hub of the United States Naval South Pacific Operations. It is also a key base for the US Air Force Strategic Air Command. Anderson Air Force Base is one of our storage stations for nuclear weapons and also a forward strike base. Located directly west of the Philippine Islands and south of Japan, Anderson is 6,100 miles from Moscow and only 2,200 miles from Vladivostok in the USSR. Most of the USSR is located between the cities of Moscow and Vladivostok, all within range of our B-36 bombers flying out of Anderson.

* * * * *

If SAC were ordered to fly its preplanned combat missions, the most likely scenario for the 6th Bomb Wing would be to take off from Walker, pick up weapons from a weapon storage airfield, and fly to a base in Alaska, Greenland, Guam, or some other forward location, and wait. This would occur if war seemed imminent. Then, when ordered, the aircraft would fly from their forward base to their assigned targets in the USSR and take part in a war with unbelievable consequences.

With the weight of nuclear weapons on board limiting our range, most of our aircraft, if surviving the bomb drop itself and the Soviet defenses, would not have enough fuel to return to airfields in continental United States. The flights would be required to land at fields in Europe, the Middle East, or Japan. While crew members are confident in their ability to deliver weapons on assigned targets, most are much less confident that they would survive the mission.

We all assume that aircraft from the USSR would, at the same time, be dropping nuclear weapons on targets in the United States. The whole scenario is grotesque and beyond reason.

* * * * *

Guam is surrounded, for security against a surprise attack, by a radar and electronic screen located many miles offshore. Every aircraft and ship must be cleared by the military on Guam before penetrating this envelope.

On our leg from Wake to Guam, our sun observations have been consistent and accurate. About 200 miles out from Guam, I call in to the flight deck with our last small heading correction, which should take us directly over the island. I also give the pilots my estimated latitude and longitude, and our ETA for penetration of the screen. The sun is shining brightly, the water a beautiful blue, almost calm, and winds are light and holding steady. Everyone on board is tired, but becomes animated and excited as we get closer. We descend slowly, and through scattered clouds below, we are finally able to see the very small and very green island paradise.

"Assume landing positions," is ordered from the flight deck and we move to our places in the radio room. I have a fleeting thought, wondering if Major Kingby was able to get enough sleep to be ready for this landing. I put my back against the forward wall in the radio room, pull up my knees, close my eyes, and hear only the roar of engines. After a long wait, I hear the landing gear slowly settle on the concrete of the runway. We have completed the flight. And we had only five engines turning part of the time.

We are on the ground. The aircraft rolls on the taxiway forever, finally shuts down at our assigned spot on the apron, and we exit the aircraft. The breeze is soft, warm, and humid. Quiet without the sound of engines. Looking in all directions, I can see lines of parked B-36 aircraft and some buildings in the distance, and dark green jungle beyond in all directions. Along with the rest of the crew, I climb back into the aircraft and prepare to unload my gear. Major

Kingby comes down from the flight deck to my station. I thought that he had already exited the aircraft, but I guess not.

"A navigation problem we need to talk about," the major says as he sits on Radar's chair five feet away from me.

There is now no one is in the radar compartment except the major and me.

"Sir?"

"Your course to Guam split the island right down the middle. Perfect. Your ETA to penetration point was slightly less than fifteen minutes off, but within limits, or we would have had a visit from interceptors. Any idea why? They didn't scramble interceptors, but I got called on it by Anderson Control Tower."

"Fifteen minutes! Damn!" I sit down. "Sun shots were good. Consistent, and they plotted well. We approached almost directly from the east and—"

Suddenly I know why! My hands come up to each side of my head, and I feel my face heat up. *Stupid! Stupid!* I look at the major, who is calmly waiting. I feel a sharp pain in my gut.

"I made a mistake and I know what it is," I tell him quietly. "We were heading directly west. I must have screwed up the computation."

I turn around at my table, pick up my book of celestial tables, and turn back to Kingby. Opening up to the page I'd been using for the last four sun shots, I look—and I know. The page lists multiple columns across the entire page.

"Looks like about two hours before Guam, I somehow moved from the proper column in the celestial tables to one column over, which would account for fifteen minutes of time error. I had been plotting the last four fixes correctly north-south but the column error put me fifteen minutes off east-west." I have nothing to add that will help." I pause. "Sorry, sir, no excuse."

Kingby continues to look at me, but he says nothing, his expression unchanged.

Finally, he says, "Error made, error found. I think the memory of this conversation will keep you from making that error again in the future."

He stands, so I stand.

I say, "I think you should know that if we were flying north-south instead of east-west, my ETA would have been right on, but I would have been about fifty miles off course. If we had a cloud deck below, no radar, and no directional radio, we could have missed the island completely and flown past. I was lucky."

"I know," he says.

He turns, steps down into radio room, out the hatch, and down the ladder to the concrete apron.

I sit back down in my chair for a while, look at nothing until the turmoil within me eases. I finally step down into the radio room and down the ladder to the concrete apron.

Chapter Ten

Tokyo R & R

Anderson Air Force Base is enormous. Neat rows of B-36's are spread over acres of concrete. At Walker, planes of the three squadrons are parked in three separate clusters. Here, they are all parked in continuous rows. *Damn impressive.* On another part of the big field sit rows of jet interceptors, and beyond the interceptors, a mix of transports. The transport aircraft, all of them, are high capacity and long range. The closest airfields are in the Philippines, too far for small aircraft with small fuel tanks.

* * * * *

I'm standing in front of our transit barracks under a big palm tree. Temperature must be ninety degrees, with a soft, moisture-laden breeze blowing across the field. My armpits are wet, and they will stay that way all day, every day. All the bachelor officer quarters are constructed of aluminum siding and aluminum roofing. All the windows stay open all day and night because the weather cools a few degrees at night, but not very much. We are each provided with a wooden locker for our clothes and shoes, and each locker contains a light bulb that remains on all day and all night. Heat from the bulb is supposed to dry out our clothes and shoes, which are always damp from the humidity, but the results are uneven. Sometimes, mold takes over very quickly.

All the other buildings I can see—the mess halls, offices, and flight line buildings—are all constructed same as our housing. We call it all "tin town." There are other buildings, constructed of concrete block, located on the far side of the runways, and we know that they are the storage buildings for dummy nuclear weapons. We also know that under those concrete block buildings, a vast tunnel system has been constructed, where the combat nuclear weapons are stored. The concrete-block buildings and tunnel system are protected by fences, motion sensors, cameras, and a unit of Air Force military police on foot and in roving patrols. Beyond the field lies a thick, impenetrable jungle. I hear that the growth of the jungle is so overpowering that it constantly creeps onto the fields and roads, and every few months has to be bulldozed to cut back the growth or else it will cover everything. The sand beaches are beautiful, with palm trees growing where sand and jungle meet. Waves are not too big or rough, but we're told that the water is home to many varieties of sharks. It seems that when a typhoon blows across the island every few years, the wind and waves are fierce and cause lots of damage. When a typhoon approaches, all aircraft on the island are flown to safe fields in the Philippines until the weather calms down. Off the sandy beaches, we can see the rusty remains of ships and landing craft still poking above the water, left there since our beach landings to take the island back from the Japanese. On the beach, empty, scattered, and ghostly forlorn, lay the shattered remains of concrete fortifications, built by the Japanese to defend the island from invasion.

JAPANESE GUNS ON THE BEACH

Everything that isn't made of concrete has been worn away by the weather or removed years before, and the remains are stark naked. Violent storms sweep over the islands every few years, and the wind and water scour and batter the concrete and gradually wear away the old fortifications. The native islanders tell us that when the Americans landed on the beaches to take the island back, the Japanese would not surrender and fought until they were killed. Many of the natives believe that ghosts of dead Japanese soldiers still roam the island after dark.

Most of roads from the base to the beaches are of gravel and are narrow. One road, wider than the others and well maintained, is the road to Agana, the only town on the island. Other small villages, most with no names, are scattered along side dirt roads all over the island. The buildings in these small villages are made up of parts of old, rusty Quonset huts or are shacks of wood with rusty scrap-metal sides and roofs.

The town of Agana is built along the beach, and the buildings are mostly of concrete block. Bars, some restaurants, and grocery and clothing stores line the streets, along with some shops selling seashells and items from the jungle and sea. Shops are owned and managed mainly by Filipinos, and we see few natives of Guam in town.

Food on the base is good. The Officers and Enlisted Men's Clubs on base have bars, and their dining rooms regularly serve fresh fish from the sea. There is little reason to go to Agana more than once just to look around, and the brown natives and the military men and their families have little reason to go downtown. I'm told that the naval facilities located on the other end of the island are extensive and first class, with large numbers of navy military families living on the base.

Our crews are kept as busy as possible by staff of the 6th Bomb Wing. Some classes, plus a training flight every ten days or so. Our training missions are relatively short, just eight- or ten-hour flights. We fly over nearby islands—like Tinian, Saipan, and Rota—simulate a bomb drop, and then make our way back to Guam.

* * * * *

Tokyo!

All crews of the 6th Bomb Wing are spending three months on a beautiful tropic island in the South Pacific called Guam. Pristine beaches, palm trees, and good food. As a reward for this "hardship" duty, all crews are allowed a two-day pass to Tokyo, 1,500 miles north of our island.

And it is our turn for Tokyo! Our crew takes off from Anderson at 0700 hours, flying our B-36 directly to Tokyo, just a six-hour flight. We are excited, as most of us have never been to Japan, and our mission is R and R—rest and relaxation. Landing at Narita Airport, the civilian airfield near Tokyo, we find that an American mess hall and base housing are located adjacent to the airport. The civilian deskman at the BOQ tells me I need to exchange my dollars for script, the currency we need to use off base. The Officers Club is a block away, and I make the exchange there with little trouble.

I board a scheduled civilian bus from the Officers Club to a tourist area that was recommended by the deskman at the BOQ, about an hour's travel time, located on the near side of Tokyo. The bus is comfortable, and crowded with military men, their dependents, and Japanese civilians who probably work on the base.

Just outside the base and tight up against the base fencing is a small, busy commercial area, and the bus moves slowly through the noisy crowds. On both sides of the street are bars, sushi restaurants, gift shops, and noodle stalls, extending for about six blocks. Prostitutes stand on most of the street corners. Leaving the activity near the gate, the countryside abruptly changes to farmland. Many farms are clustered fairly close to the road. Women tend the small plots, and they are dressed in brown trousers and jackets and conical straw hats with straps under their chins. The plots are neat, well cared for, and green, growing what looks like a variety of garden vegetables.

The road is busy and crowded with noisy small cars, bicycles of every kind, scooters, motorbikes, and small trucks, but the fields beyond seem peaceful. The bus takes me to the Ginza tourist district: noisy, colorful, exciting, and inviting.

Dressed in Western clothing, school uniforms, or colorful traditional garments, the Japanese in Ginza contrast sharply with the drab browns and tans worn by the Japanese from the countryside who are probably new to the city. Everyone, including men, women, and even the school children, seems to be hurrying to get to somewhere important.

Neon signs, it seems, cover every possible surface. The time is about 1600 hours now. All the shop windows are lit up, and young girls, in traditional Japanese dress, stand on the sidewalk in front of the shops, urging me toward their stores with their hands, body movements, and radiant smiles. The front windows of restaurants, sushi bars, and noodle shops display the foods they serve inside. The displays look inviting but are made of plastic, shaped and colored to look real and appealing. Traffic clogs the street, horns honk, and the vehicles move slowly or not at all.

I stand on the wide sidewalk with my back against one of the few solid walls between shops, and just watch and listen, fascinated. The adults do not make eye contact, and whether dressed in Western or traditional Japanese clothes, they look down at the sidewalk when they pass close to me. I'm sure the adults still remember very well that we are part of a foreign military force occupying their homeland. I am in uniform.

Teenage girls, already in groups of three or four, are dressed in their school uniforms of modest blue skirts, white shirts, and sneakers. They always make eye contact, smile, say something to their friends, cover their mouths, and giggle. What fun! Children, pulled along by their mothers, stare up at me. Their mothers continue to look down. Many adult women wear colorful kimonos, and wooden shoes with a strap, and their shoes make a distinctive, rhythmic tap-tap on the brick sidewalk. Most of the men wear traditional Western clothing along with leather shoes, and some young women wear modern Western clothing and sneakers. T-shirts are popular with the young people, while suits, vests, and ties are preferred by the older men. They present a wonderful mix of color and sound, traditional and new, all blending in harmony. Japan is a country in the torture of massive change, and it is evident everywhere.

I'm hungry and want to eat before boarding the bus back to Narita Field. The window of one of the many small restaurants has a display of different kinds of noodles in bowls. Looking through the front door, I see Japanese people seated at little tables inside. I catch the eye of one of the kimono-clad waitresses, who at first looks down, but then turns her face up to lock eyes with me. I smile and wave for her to come out the front door to the window display. She does so, and I point at a blue bowl in the window, filled with noodles, shrimp, and what looks like seaweed. Of course the display is plastic. The pretty little woman smiles, bows, and motions for me to follow her into the restaurant. I sit at a small table, and before I can even settle in, the waitress places a steaming bowl of soup in front of me. The bowl of soup looks just like the one in the window, plus I also have a plastic spoon and wooden chopsticks in a paper sleeve. I look around, watch, and then mimic what I see. I lift the bowl to my face, push noodles into my mouth, and slurp loudly like everyone else. People sitting close by look up, nod, and smile in approval. The food is delicious and filling. I eat slowly and soak up the atmosphere of the scene. After a while, when I am finished, I step up to the cashier. I again smile and hold out script in my flat hand. The woman at the register, a little older than the waitress, delicately and carefully picks out a bill and returns two coins, again with a smile. The bus to Narita is crowded and I stand all the way to the back, very pleased with myself.

Each crew is scheduled to spend only one night in Narita. We have tomorrow morning free, but will be picked up at the BOQ at 1600 hours for the return flight to Anderson. I'll come back tomorrow morning to soak up more of the Ginza tourist scene. Maybe someday, I will return to see the real Japan behind the smiles and traditional facade that is set in place for the tourists.

Our war with Japan ended in 1945. Was it just nine years ago? I wonder if, behind the smiles, there is a profound sadness and maybe a hostility from a war lost and military occupancy by a winning, mostly white American army. Nagasaki? Hiroshima? Brutal killing of opposing armies on both sides only several years ago—and now smiling friends. The human species is flawed.

* * * * *

The flight back to Guam the next day is uneventful. On board, there is a lot of excited conversation about a culture most of us had never been exposed to before. Of course, our short exposure has been as tourists. There is a depth to Japan that someday I would like to find, explore, and know.

We land at Anderson after dark. As the aircraft taxis to our parking spot, the crew opens as many hatches as possible to the night air, which we do at the end of each flight to pick up any cooling breeze that we can find. Besides the noise of the engines, just above idle to move us slowly down the field, is a continuous stream of loud, crunching noises from below. We find that the paved areas of the field are covered with thousands of giant snails, each the size of a man's fist, which come out of the jungle only after dark. The crunching noise is from the aircraft tires rolling over and crushing snail shells. The Japanese soldiers brought the snails from home, a favorite food in Japan, when they occupied Guam during the war. The snails liked the jungle and multiplied quickly. No one knows why the snails remain in the jungle all day but venture out onto the acres of concrete and asphalt paving when the sun goes down. The Japanese might have gone home, but the snails remain and continue to multiply.

After seeing the beaches, the town of Agana, and the small villages scattered along the dirt roads in the jungle, Guam has become routine. The natives stay away from all the Navy and Air Force military, and live their lives apart from the vast number of probably unwelcomed visitors. Our Air Force personnel, permanent and on rotation, do not mix much with the Navy on the island, either. There has been a longstanding difference of opinion, at the highest levels, between the Strategic Air Command and the Navy about the ability of B-36 aircraft to drop nuclear weapons on the USSR if it becomes necessary. During most of the Cold War thus far, the Navy has had no system that could deliver a nuclear weapon against an enemy—and service rivalry remains strong. The disagreement has filtered down through the ranks. It was decided, with only conditional agreement by the Navy, again at the highest levels, that the B-36 aircraft is the best and only system we have that can place nuclear bombs on an enemy. At this time, the B-36 is our deterrent weapon during these Cold War years. The Navy understands. This is the best we have today. The B-36 is our Cold War Shield.

Chapter Eleven

Over Manila

One morning, our crew is called for a briefing by our squadron commander and told that we will be one of three B-36 aircraft flying to Manila the next day. The Philippine Islands are located directly west of Guam, and our crew welcomes the change. Most of our training flights have been north and sometimes east. Manila is 1,600 miles from Guam and our flight time will be about seven hours. The reason for the flight, though, is not disclosed.

The following morning, our B-36 and two others from our wing prepare to fly to the Philippine Islands. Takeoff time is at 0630 hours, and the six and a half-hour flight to the islands is uneventful. On the lower deck, we have no specific navigation or radar requirements to be met during the flight, which is unusual. We pass over Manila at 20,000 feet, flying not too close to the other two planes, but still in visual contact. Continuing on past Manila, all three aircraft start a descent, and, at the same time, the other two B-36's change position. We on the lower deck are watching and can't believe what is happening. The aircraft form a line! We are now second in a line of three. This is not a landing pattern. The aircraft shorten the distances between them and we are in the middle of this so-called formation, which is looking pretty dangerous to me. I have heard quite often from pilots that the B-36 is slow to respond to changes of the controls, so flying a tight formation with two other elephants doesn't seem like a good idea to me. The lead aircraft starts a 180-degree turn while losing altitude rapidly and we follow close behind. I look around at the other faces on our lower deck, and everybody is holding on to structure just as I am. We increase our speed and fly closer to the lead aircraft!

TO MANILA FLYOVER

Is the third B-36 following us? We are close and low, moving at a high rate of speed, and our aircraft is being buffeted by ground turbulence. The engines are screaming and all jets are online. *What the hell is going on?* The only other time we have flown this low is over a runway while taking off, or landing—and not at this high speed. Not a word from the flight deck. They must be pretty busy right now. I am sitting in my navigator's chair, holding on to structure and looking forward through the greenhouse. *Unbelievable!* We are flying over rural land, and the ground is flashing below us. I feel a familiar pain in my gut and it's not from choppy air: it's pure fear.

I turn and look at Panetta. He is holding on, eyes wide open. I imagine I look the same. Radar is staring into his radar set eye-shield and holding on to his desktop. I can see only the back of his head—and he looks rigid. The engines roar and scream. We are heading down and increasing speed. The rural countryside quickly changes to cityscape. I am able to see more detail on the ground than I want, but we are moving so fast that everything on the ground is a blur. I want to close my eyes and give up, but I don't. I just can't take my eyes away from the ground rushing below. *Insane.* The nose of the plane suddenly rises sharply at a steep angle as we fly over a runway, too fast and too low. All ten engines must be full-out, the noise deafening. My stomach is knotted up. *Son of a bitch!*

Three B-36 aircraft have just made a flyover at Manila Airport! There must be a gathering of bigwigs on the ground at the airport, and the Strategic Air Command of the United States Air Force decided to make a military and a national display of power. All three planes flew in low and loud and out. *Damn.* We are still climbing. The assholes on the flight deck of course knew we were going to do a flyover and didn't bother to tell the rest of us. *Bet they are laughing their asses off right now, probably falling out of their seats.* Lots of fun for them and they have a story to tell over beers at the O Club.

After all that, our flight back to Anderson is routine.

General LeMay uses every opportunity to show off his B-36's to the public, the USSR, and probably the US Navy. That is what this was all about. Manila must have been celebrating a special day or occasion, and LeMay saw the opportunity to show them and the world his "big stick" up close.

Chapter Twelve

Bangkok—Forget It

Our stay in Guam has become boring after a few weeks. The beaches are beautiful to look at the first time and even the second time, but that is enough. The islanders remain distant, and the training flights routine. We all send and receive letters and photos to and from home, but time drags anyway. Thanksgiving arrives and is gone. On Thanksgiving Day, we all eat turkey and cranberries in the mess hall. The weather is eighty-five degrees and muggy all day. Three months from our departure in mid September will get us home a couple of weeks before Christmas. We shall see. The days pass.

People say that we really have little control over our lives. Luck, circumstances, and emotional decisions seem to take control at times. *Sure seems that way.* I never thought that I would ever see the island of Guam.

I graduated from a college in upstate New York, far away from the excitement of the big cities. With my family living in California, I was pretty much on my own. The Korean War was dragging on, and fresh from graduation, I found myself a job working as an engineer for a company on Long Island that made airplane parts. The job didn't hold much interest for me, but it provided a deferment that was keeping me out of the military draft for three months. Still, I wasn't happy with my life.

One Saturday morning, I took a train to New York and then a subway to Times Square. I had always been attracted to the bright lights and the hurry of Times Square, and remembered that there was an all-services military recruiting station located in the heart of Times Square. Making one of those emotional decisions that so easily beat back logic, I walked in and enlisted for a four-year tour in the Air Force. Dumb? Never thought it was dumb. Turned out to be one of the most important and better decisions of my life.

Within three weeks, I started basic training at Sampson Air Force Base located in upstate New York. While I was still in basic training, I applied for an opportunity to be part of a flight crew. The Air Force gave me a battery of tests, said I qualified to train as a navigator, and then they sent me to an Air Cadet program at Ellington Air Force Base in Texas. After completing the Air Cadet program, I was assigned to Navigator School at Mather Air Force Base in California. Months later, I graduated from Mather as an officer and a navigator, and I received orders to report to Walker Air Force Base in Roswell, New Mexico. Walker Air Force Base was the home of the 6th Bomb Wing, part of the Strategic Air Command, and I was assigned as Navigator on a B-36 aircraft. Exciting? Yes. Good life? You bet. At that time, most flight crew officers were a product of West Point, the Air Force Academy, or college ROTC programs. I was what the Air Force called a "mustang," having first served as an enlisted man and then as an officer.

* * * * *

Crew briefing on this day is held at 0900 hours. Unusual, since we just completed a training flight just two days before.

At the briefing, Major Kingby tells us, "We are scheduled for a flight tomorrow morning departing at 0600 hours. This is not a training flight but what Wing calls a 'utility mission.' We will be flying one full day out, will have two nights on the ground, and then a full day flight to return. Bring whatever you need for two nights in civilian housing. No other uniform required except a change of flight suit. You will carry full gear and equipment as for a standard training mission, but we will have no in-flight training requirements to fulfill. Destination and details will be provided tomorrow morning.

Everyone will meet here at the flight building at 0430 hours for transportation to the aircraft. Any questions? Good. Lieutenant Hall, we need to talk for a few minutes. Dismissed."

When we are alone, Major Kingby says, "Hall, this information for tomorrow's flight is on a 'need to know only.'"

He hands me a single sheet of paper showing a reduced copy of our flight plan—to Bangkok, Thailand!

My heart gives a leap, but I work hard to keep my expression neutral. Never been to that part of the world. Exotic Thailand!

Major Kingby then says, "You need to plot a flight to Bangkok that is pretty close to the flight plan shown on this sheet, which has been prepared by Wing staff. Lay out a flight plan, compute no-wind headings and flight times for each leg. I will meet you here at 1400 hours to review your work, and I will keep your charts and numbers so that I can submit them for Wing's approval. I will return your charts and flight plan to you tomorrow morning at the aircraft. See you at 1400 hours."

"Yes, sir."

Why the hell is our crew flying a "need to know only" mission to Bangkok? Have other crews flown to Thailand, and because we did not have a need to know, we never heard about it? Maybe it's our turn in an operation that has been ongoing that no one is talking about?

I retrieve my map case from my locker and go to see Sergeant Delaney, who works in Operations.

"Sergeant, for a few hours, I need a desk or tabletop with good lighting. I have to lay out a flight plan and I want no interruptions and no one looking over my shoulder. I'm meeting with Major Kingby at 1400 hours and need to have my flight plan ready by then. Any idea where I might find an empty table or desk?"

"No problem, Lieutenant. I have a small office that is empty except for one chair and one desk. Lighting is okay. Please follow me."

The room has no windows, but the lighting is adequate and I am happy to have a desk in a location where no one will bother me. I already have the necessary charts in my case. I need to remember to replace the charts that I'm taking from by case with new ones when we get back.

Using the information given to me by Major Kingby, I plot a route west over the Philippines, then southwest over the South China

Sea, northwest into the Gulf of Thailand, and then plot a dogleg into Bangkok. I work up headings, distances, and times on each leg, assuming a no-wind condition. Done. I have plenty of time before I'm to meet Major Kingby at 1400 hours. I pack up my charts and papers, lock the office with the key that the efficient Sergeant Delaney has provided me and, with case in hand, go out for coffee and a sandwich.

Thirty minutes later, I return to the office, pull out my plotted charts and flight plan, and check all I had done. Then, without referring to the numbers I had already run, I again prepare headings, distances, and times on each leg. I check the first set with the second and find no errors. The total distance is 3,400 miles, and I estimate 15.5 hours of flight time. A takeoff at 0600 would bring us into Bangkok at 2130 hours. I return the key to Sergeant Delaney, express my thanks, and then sit outside of the Squadron Flight Line Building on a concrete block wall for half an hour. At 1400 hours, I look for Major Kingby. He is at a corner table in the briefing room, and I hand him my proposed flight information. I sit quietly as he scans my charts and papers.

"Looks good to me," he says. "I'm on my way to Wing right now, and their staff navigator will review your flight plan. I will call you here at Operations before 1600 hours to notify you of their approval, and then I will hold onto your charts and calculations until morning. Will see you here at 0410 hours tomorrow morning for a weather briefing. Good work. I expect no problems at Wing. Remember, no one else has a need to know at this time."

I wait in Operations, and at 1535 hours, I receive a call from Major Kingby telling me that all is approved and again confirming that we will meet for weather briefing at 0410 tomorrow morning.

The next morning, we are at the weather counter for a briefing at 0415, just Major Kingby and me. We find that we are going to have moderate winds aloft and broken cloud cover above and below our 22,000-foot planned flight altitude.

Major Kingby arranges for transportation, and at 0500 hours, we meet the rest of our crew at the nose wheel assembly of our aircraft. We form two lines, facing Major Kingby for briefing.

"As I outlined yesterday, Wing staff is calling our flight today a 'utility mission.' Our bomb bays are packed with pallets loaded with military hardware that we shall carry to Bangkok and transfer as ordered. Our planned altitude for the flight is at 22,000 feet. Shortly after takeoff, I will provide additional information. Fly safe and stay alert. Navigator, I have a packet for you. Let's get to it."

Major Kingby hands me my charts and flight plan, and we all get to work. As soon as I get to my station, I check the packet to make sure I have all my charts and flight information, and then, using the data from our weather briefing, determine an initial heading to relay to the flight deck after takeoff.

Panetta and I complete our preflight check lists.

"What the hell is going on?" Panetta asks me. "No information, one flight, two nights' rest, and return? Everyone on the crew has his own theory."

"Kingby said he would bring everyone up to date right after takeoff. Best to wait and get the information directly from the major," is my non-answer.

For some reason I feel guilty. Panetta wants to know what is happening. I know some information and I can't tell him the little I know. *Needs to wait for Kingby. Best to keep my mouth shut.*

With all preflights complete, Kingby rolls our aircraft down the taxi strip to the runway, makes a clean takeoff at 0620 hours, and starts a climb to 22,000 feet. I call the flight deck with an initial heading of two seven five degrees.

"Crew, this is Major Kingby. Everyone on intercom."

Pause.

"We are on our way to Bangkok in Thailand. Bangkok is 3,400 miles directly west of Guam on mainland Asia. Estimate of flight time is fifteen and one-half hours. Two days ago, I received orders from Wing through Squadron Operations to prepare for this flight. We are ferrying a full bomb bay load of military cargo to a US Army unit stationed in Bangkok. Our orders state that no one is to have information about our flight unless that person has a need to know. Yesterday, Lieutenant Hall prepared a flight plan for Wing's approval, which was obtained. Our orders tell us that after we return to Guam, we are to discuss this flight with no one at any time unless Wing gives written approval. That means that upon our return to Guam, we forget that this flight ever happened. Your activities on the ground in Bangkok will be very limited. Kingby out."

"Panetta," I say, "take a sun shot when we level off and the plane holds steady."

Panetta doesn't look happy to be going to Thailand. He's never been there, but it sounds as if we aren't going to see much of the country. Since we won't have any free time in Bangkok, I'm no longer very happy about the flight myself. Long flight, all over water, time on the ground to sleep and eat, and then a long flight back.

I bring Panetta and Major Heller up to date about our planned flight. Our first leg is to Manila, then a turn southwest to the most southerly of the Spratly Islands in the South China Sea, west again to a point in the middle of the Gulf of Thailand, and then north to Bangkok. The flight would be shorter if we flew Manila direct to Bangkok, but that would take us over Vietnam and Cambodia, and instructions from Wing stated that we are to avoid the airspace over those two countries.

Winds are light and cloud cover is broken on top and 50-percent coverage below. Panetta takes sun readings every thirty minutes and they plot well. About two hours out of Anderson, I call the flight deck with a ten-degree correction. Winds are holding steady.

What are we doing delivering military cargo to Thailand? Do we have American military personnel in Thailand, or is this a delivery for Thai troops? I haven't heard about any activities in Thailand, but I guess the president doesn't feel he needs to keep me up to date. I don't think I'm on his "need to know" list. I wonder if the Chinese are pushing south toward Thailand?

We fly over Quezon City and Manila at 1314 hours. It has been an uneventful flight so far, and I hope it stays that way. Boring is good. Radar checks out Manila.

"Navigator to Pilot."

"Pilot."

"New heading two two five degrees to Spratly Islands"

"Pilot, turning to two two five degrees."

We have a little more than three hours until we reach the Spratly Islands. On my chart, Spratly looks like a group of small volcanic and coral islands scattered over a wide area. Not the best landmark for us to use as a turn point, but there is not much else in this part of the South China Sea.

"Navigator to Radar."

"This is Radar."

"Radar, I have an ETA to Spratly Islands of 1645 hours. Appreciate if you can check them out about that time. The islands are small and scattered, and if I miss them, we'll end up in Singapore."

"Radar, understand 1645 hours."

We continue toward the rocks in the China Sea. We have no training requirements to fulfill on any of the legs, and the flight remains quiet and boring. Uneventful. I like it. Panetta and I shoot the sun, plot, and call in small changes in heading.

When I ask Snell at radio about condition of the aircraft, as I do periodically, he tells me that engine number four is losing oil. Number four is still online, he says, but they will be shutting it down in a few minutes. Everything else looks good. A steady reassuring drone continues to fill every corner of the lower deck.

Time is 1605 hours, and the sun is still high enough for sightings, but Panetta and I are crowding the greenhouse looking for any rocks in the sea we can label as Spratly. Sun readings say that we are close to planned course. Time is 1615, and I ask Panetta to shoot the sun. I stay at the greenhouse still looking for Spratly rocks. Panetta says they are good readings, and I plot. The fix is just short of where the islands should be, but looking out the greenhouse, I see nothing but blue water.

Radar peers into his scope and says nothing. *Shit.* I would really like to see a little bit of rock. Panetta is at the greenhouse and says he sees nothing, and I prepare a new heading to call in to the flight deck.

"Navigator to Pilot."

"Pilot here."

"Navigator to Pilot. New heading now two seven two degrees."

"Pilot, heading two seven two degrees."

The right wing dips smoothly as we turn. I crouch down at the greenhouse as we complete the turn, still looking for a rock in the blue, blue sea.

"Radar to Navigator, I see two small rocks close in at about eleven o'clock. I forgot that you wanted me to call you."

He turns, looking at Panetta and me with a broad, toothy grin. We made his day. He just wanted us to work up a sweat.

"Shit, Bob," I say on the intercom, "you probably have been looking at islands for the last twenty minutes. Forgot, hell! I guess you must be getting pretty old … sir."

I can't hear them, but I imagine the rest of the crew are having a good laugh with Radar. Panetta peers at the radar screen over Heller's shoulder to look at the islands.

"Shit," he says, echoing my sentiments.

I'm surprised Kingby didn't ask for intercom discipline. Too busy laughing, I guess. I never did see those rocks. I guess if they have no green growth on them, the gray rocks blend in pretty well with the blue ocean. I guess.

This leg we're flying is 700 miles long into the Sea of Thailand, about a three-hour leg. We'll lose the sun in about one hour, and then we will be flying blind for thirty or forty minutes. The sun is dead ahead, bright through the greenhouse window, and filling the radar compartment with an uncomfortable glare.

"Panetta," I call, "let's take a sun shot in twenty minutes from now and another as late as possible before we lose it."

"No problem," Panetta says. "I'll be in the radio room for twenty minutes."

I eat a frigid turkey sandwich from my white flight lunch box and drink a bottle of water, followed by fruit cocktail, a candy bar, and more water. I'm up and off intercom to look for Panetta. I find him sound asleep in the radio room. I let him sleep, and I take the sun reading myself and plot it on my chart. Panetta sleeps for ten more minutes, and I call Snell and ask him to wake Panetta. He staggers in and sits at the nav station.

"Take our last reading as late as possible so we can plot and figure a wind to carry us through the blind time. Call me," I say.

"No problem," he responds.

I sit on the floor of the radio room on some lumpy bags but I'm wide awake.

But then Snell nudges me. I actually fell asleep. Panetta has already taken the last sun reading. Through the greenhouse, we see the glowing sun is just about to set in the water. I look over Panetta's shoulder as he plots the fix.

"Call in a correction to the gulf turn point and I'll sit in during our blind time," I say.

Panetta calls for a five-degree correction and gives up the nav seat. I spend some time cleaning up the chart and log.

I'm sure that Wing staff is going to take a good look at our charts and log from this "utility mission" when we get back. If I clean up the paperwork, Wing might get the impression that we know what the hell we are doing. *Maybe.*

We have front-row seats to watch a colorful South Pacific sunset through our greenhouse window. Very pretty. I should carry a camera. Photos from within a B-36 in flight? Not allowed.

I dead-reckon through our blind time, and the sky darkens. We need at least a two-star fix before our turn over the gulf.

Panetta shouts, "I'm going up to the dome."

He climbs up to the dome, knowing it is too early, but I guess waiting at the dome is just as good as waiting in the radar room. After a long wait, the sky finally darkens enough for Panetta to find three target stars, and he comes down with a three-star set. I plot them.

"Looks good, Paul. We are off track about twelve miles north of course. Not enough for a correction now, but we'll call in a change of heading after our next fix."

Twenty five minutes later, Panetta sights through about 30-percent cloud cover above and completes another set of star sightings. The fix plots eighteen miles north of course. Since our next turn will be to the north, we hold our present heading until we intersect with our northbound planned track, and we'll will make our turn then.

"Navigator to Pilot."

"Pilot"

"New heading three five zero degrees to Bangkok. ETA 2120 hours."

"Pilot. Understand three five zero degrees."

We are now over the middle of the Gulf of Thailand with less than two hours remaining to Bangkok. We take three more star plots spaced at about thirty minutes apart. It looks like we are going to have heavy fog along the coast. I can see the lights of a few small towns as the gulf narrows just before Bangkok, which must be a good-sized city, because the glow of lights is strong through the fog. We start a slow descent through the fog.

"Pilot to Scanners."

"Left-side Scanner here."

131

"Scanners, be alert. The airport at Bangkok is a combined civil- and military-use field. Probably lots of traffic. Look for small private planes that think there is no one else in the sky but them. Military aircraft might fly close just to take a good look at a B-36."

"Scanner, understand. Scanners on the job."

As we descend, we break out of the bottom of the fog layer and fly into a clear sky. Bangkok at night is full of lights—colors of gold and red, many shades of white, and the glitz of thousands of multicolored neon signs in the center of the city. It is late in the evening, but from the air as we descend, the city looks alive, vibrant, and exotic. Temple spires and gardens are lit up, and we can see that downtown is busy and crowded.

"Crew, this is Flight Deck. We are entering the landing pattern. Take landing positions."

"Radar, will comply."

"Chief Gunner, will comply."

As I move to the radio room, I look back through the greenhouse, and I can see a very large airport with lighted runways in the center and many buildings on both sides of the runway pattern.

A slick landing follows, and when we are close to a taxiway, two camouflaged jeeps, carrying three armed soldiers each, take positions at each wingtip, and they escort us along the taxiway to the parking apron. They are there to make sure that our wingtips are clear and also to monitor our plane itself. Across the runways, I can see the civilian airport, modern and busy. We are obviously on the military side, and this side is not well lit, and is cold and hard. The apron is crowded with all types of aircraft, including many helicopters, all painted in camouflage patterns. Soldiers on foot and in moving jeeps form a protective net around the parked military aircraft.

After engine shutdown, we remain at our stations and watch as another jeep pulls up to the nose of our plane. Our aircraft commander and second pilot exit down the forward compartment ladder and walk toward the jeep.

The passenger in the jeep, a military man dressed in camouflage, climbs out of the vehicle, comes to attention, and salutes Major Kingby when he comes close. Major Kingby returns the salute and they all talk quietly.

A large bus, also painted in camouflage, approaches our plane. Major Kingby and Captain Harris return to the aircraft. Captain Harris, using Radio's headset, tells the members of our crew to offload, bringing all our gear, and to form up at the nose wheel.

We exit the aircraft and form two lines at the nose.

Major Kingby tells us, "I spoke to a US Army officer from the local detachment; he came in the jeep. The bus will transport us to a building on the flight line, where I will check us in, then we will be transported to a hotel in Bangkok. We will be having dinner at a restaurant in the hotel, and we will be restricted to the hotel as long as we are on the ground. This hotel, in effect, is the US Army living quarters for visiting civilian and military personnel. There are military police at each exit, and they are in place to make sure no one enters or leaves the building. All our meals will be provided at the hotel, and the dining room is open twenty-four hours a day. A bus will pick us up in front of the hotel tomorrow night at 2345 hours to transport us back to the airfield. We will depart for Guam immediately after weather briefing and preflight. Any questions?"

None.

We board the bus, and it carries us through the heart of Bangkok. The driver is Thai, and I guess he knows, from past similar situations, that we are not going to see much of Bangkok except through the windows of his bus. The time is 2230 hours local, but the streets are crowded with people and traffic as we drive through the city center. The weather is warm, and the people, both men and women, are dressed in trousers and colorful tops.

Our driver calls out, "Grand Palace," and points to a walled area to the right—the walls white, doors red, and all floodlit. Many of the buildings have green- or orange-colored tiled roofs, conical spires, and pediments, and they are all floodlit. Some spires are golden.

"Temple Emerald Buddha," sings out the driver a few minutes later as we pass a brightly lit group of temple buildings, protecting I guess, an emerald Buddha. "Buddhist temples are called 'wats,'" he says as he points.

Our hotel is "international style" and could be located in any big city in the world. We won't be doing much here except to sleep, eat, read, and look out the windows at as much of the local scene as we can see.

133

* * * * *

At 2355 hours the following night, we board the same bus for a ride back to the airfield. The important buildings are still floodlit, but the streets are quiet. Last night at about this same hour, the streets were alive with people and activity. We wonder why but never get an answer to our question.

Security at the airfield is tight. Thai troops are stationed at the gates, outside the buildings, and on the field, and they are all carrying automatic weapons. No Americans in sight. We wait in the bus while Major Kingby and Captain Harris spend some time in the flight line building. They are getting a weather briefing and securing departure clearances, we guess. The ever-present white box lunches are loaded onto our plane from a small van, and there is little other activity on the field. Our AC and second pilot return, and Major Kingby stands at the front of the bus near the driver.

"This will be our briefing. For this flight, weather looks good all the way back. I have approved the navigator's planned route to Anderson. Route is the same as inbound to Bangkok, except we will overfly the Spratly Islands and continue east until we reach the coast of the Philippines and then turn north to Manila. At the aircraft, complete your normal preflight, and we will depart as soon as we are cleared. Bangkok is not equipped to provide maintenance on our model of aircraft, so we will take off with number four feathered. Questions? No?"

Kingby nods to the driver.

* * * * *

The jeep and Army officer who met us when we landed now follow our bus to our B-36, where he parks and waits while we make ready to fly. Just before engine start up, the jeep moves closer to our aircraft, where the officer and Major Kingby can lock eyes. The officer climbs out of his jeep, comes to attention near the nose of the B-36, and salutes. Major Kingby returns the salute from the flight deck. With an empty bomb bay, we take off with engine number four offline but causing no problems.

I wonder how many other crews from Guam have made this low-profile flight carrying arms and munitions to Bangkok. We wouldn't have heard about it, since I imagine all the people who have made this kind of delivery were told, as we were, "Forget you ever made the flight."

The United States is in Thailand conducting military activities in secret. Maybe we will hear about it some months from now. Maybe not. Forget it.

We climb through the darkness, and I call the flight deck with a heading to take us south over the Gulf of Thailand. We have no cloud cover above, and we navigate by the stars. All is well. After a 110-minute leg over the Gulf of Thailand, we turn while still over the gulf to a heading of zero eight five degrees heading toward the Philippine Islands. Star observations plot well, and then, unexpectedly, we fly into a significant wind shift.

We correct our heading after each fix to stay close to our planned flight path. Time moves slowly and we each do our job. We continue with routine star navigation until the sun rises directly in front of our aircraft, and gradually our stars fade away.

I have my sunglasses on, but the glare through the greenhouse is blinding. I set a piece of cardboard on my nav table as a temporary screen against the sun so I can see my chart. Panetta is asleep and I wait out our blind time until the sun is high enough for us to shoot for a fix. Dead reckoning is all we have till then.

The sun rises. Panetta takes sun readings and then sits in for me. Time is 0650, and I stand behind Radar and look over his shoulder at his scope.

"We should be flying over the Spratly Islands about now. See any rocks in the ocean?" I ask Major Heller.

He smiles at me and points to two small returns on the scope. "Over Spratly now, but I didn't think you wanted a heads-up. They don't look like much on the scope."

"I'm always happy to know we're not just wandering aimlessly over the Pacific," I say. "We should be turning north in about one hour, just short of Banggi Island at the southern tip of the Philippine Islands."

I give him a high-five, pat him on the shoulder, smile, and move on. Panetta takes a second set of sun shots and waves me over to take a look.

He points to the chart and says, "After dead-reckoning through our blind time, we're fifty miles south of our planned course. Do you want to make a correction or let it play out?"

"Why don't you let it play out and turn north when we are abeam of Banggi, and call for a heading to Manila," I reply.

When we are directly south of Banggi, Panetta calls the pilot.

"Navigator to Pilot."

"Pilot."

"Navigator. Turn to a heading of zero four two degrees to Manila," Panetta calls.

"Pilot. Turning to heading of zero four two degrees."

Ten minutes after the turn, Panetta points out the greenhouse and yells to me, "Over Banggi Island."

I smile and give him a thumbs-up. Manila is about two and a half hours out. I read the sun, and Panetta plots and calls for corrections. Looking out the greenhouse, we can finally see Manila directly ahead.

I have heard Manila referred to as the "Pearl of the Orient," and it is located on Luzon, one of the bigger islands. From the air, Manila looks like a large and modern city, with a thriving seaport. It appears to have other towns and cities close by, and they all blend in together to cover a large area.

We close in on Manila, and the time is 1040 hours. Panetta calls the flight deck with a new heading of zero nine five degrees. The pilot completes his turn, and I trade places with Panetta. He retreats to the radio room, and we start on our last and longest leg directly to Guam. I will be glad to get back. I eat canned peaches, some kind of cold berry muffin, and decide to skip the fried chicken. I continue to drink lots of water to hold off dehydration. I'll have some chicken later, maybe.

The Pacific is calm, the sky overhead is clear with just scattered clouds, and the sun is bright and reflecting off the water. Looks like a 25-percent broken deck of clouds below.

I'm sorry I ate that cold berry muffin. It sits like a dead weight in my stomach. We will be at Anderson at about 1800 hours, and I'm look forward to a beer and a good dinner.

I take celestial readings, plot, and try to relax. Major Heller is still at the radar, but he sits without moving, and I think he is sleeping.

He tracked our position as we traveled along the west side of the islands from Banggi to Manila. Nothing to see now but surface clutter reflected from the sea.

The engines drone on. Sergeant Snell relays to me that all is normal on the flight deck with number four still offline.

I feel bored and tired, but at the same time, I'm grateful that, so far, no problems. Some men in the squadron say that the B-36 is hard on the crew. Uncomfortable, considering how long our flights usually are. I wouldn't know. I have no experience in any other type of aircraft to compare with, except the C-47's we flew in while training in Cadets. Idle thoughts.

Panetta and I have been trading off using the celestial dome and plotting. We are about one hour out of Anderson, and the sun is behind us. Our aircraft has successfully penetrated the Guam radar security envelope, matching our estimated time and location within limits. Kingby is in the radio room chatting with Sergeant Snell and, more importantly, stretching and relaxing before it's time for him to take over the controls and make ready for a landing.

Through the greenhouse, I can see some lights from the Guam naval base. It really looks like an enormous installation. The base is a major part of the Navy's South Pacific system.

Panetta has taken our last sun sighting, and our course looks good. The B-36 is now in a slow descent to landing-pattern altitude. Almost home. *Home?* Well, a home away from home.

I guess I can now claim that I've been to Bangkok and have seen some of the tourist attractions in Bangkok from a distance while looking through the window of a bus and hotel room. A flight to remember—and, as ordered, a flight to forget.

Chapter Thirteen

Flight Home

Date is the first of December. Weather in Guam hasn't changed much at all. What has changed is that everyone is thinking about flying home. Talk is that the 39th Squadron, first to leave Walker, will be the first to depart Guam. Standard procedure. Sounds fair.

Maintenance is working long hours making all our aircraft ready for the flight to Walker, and everyone keeps checking long-range weather forecasts. Letters from home are about preparing for Christmas and our return. When we flew from Walker, all of our aircraft left within a three-day period. The return, we are told, will be scheduled over two weeks. General LeMay now knows that the 6th Bomb Wing can, if we have to, get all aircraft off the ground in a three-day push; we did that at Walker. Our return will be a little more relaxed to ease up on maintenance scheduling at Anderson and ground activities at Walker.

A couple of days later, the unofficial—meaning that it will probably change—word is that the 39th Squadron will depart Anderson starting on 7 December, with five aircraft departing each day. That would mean that the 24th Squadron, being last to arrive, would be scheduled to fly out much later in December.

The mess halls and clubs are decked out in artificial Christmas trees and holiday decorations, mainly for the poor souls in the permanent party left to celebrate the holiday in the eighty-five degree, sunny, moist weather on Guam.

The next B-36 wing to deploy to Guam is expected to arrive on the island the second week in January. Their forward planning team will fly in on 22 December. Our crew is scheduled to fly out on 21 December.

At 0800 hours, on 20 December, Major Kingby holds a briefing for our crew and we are ready, more than ready, to start for home.

After Major Kingby's comments, I brief the navigation aspects of our return trip: "Our flight back to Walker will be a reverse of our flight out. We are scheduled to depart from Anderson at 0820 hours, flying over Wake Island, then Honolulu, San Diego, Phoenix, and into Walker. With a takeoff scheduled for 0820 tomorrow and with a light tailwind, we will be in the air for twenty-nine hours and plan to arrive at Walker at 1350 hours for a daylight landing. Distance is seven thousand one hundred miles."

Major Kingby closes with, "Major Heller and I will pick up the latest weather and meet you all at the flight line building at 0600 hours, ready to go."

* * * * *

I have a good breakfast, light on the solid foods, and the sky is clear. At the aircraft, everyone has plenty of time to carefully preflight, load flight bags, and make ready. The bomb bays carry only the squadron's light vehicles, our Tokyo purchases, and our personal gear.

Lots of chatter in the radio compartment as we sit with our backs against the forward bulkhead ready for takeoff.

We lift off at 0755 hours, and I call in our first heading of zero seven two degrees toward the atoll of Wake Island. Panetta and I take our sun shots, and the winds are light and steady from the west as forecast. With a light tailwind, our flight home should be a little less than time in the air than our flight to Guam from Walker. I'm happy that I am not assigned as permanent party at Anderson Air Force Base. Permanent station at Anderson means being assigned a two-year tour, and I heard that some men become depressed even on the island paradise, with too much of every day the same as yesterday.

Roswell certainly is not an ideal town to call home. Hot weather most of the year, blowing sand all year long, and located in a fairly remote part of New Mexico. At Walker, we say that we are 200 miles from anywhere, but 200 miles is really not so bad. We have a movie theater and bowling lanes on base, the food served in the mess halls and clubs is good, and the beer at the bars in the clubs is cold, cheap, and social. We can drive to Roswell for a change of scenery, Mexican food, Mexican music, and a beer among the locals. Most families live on base, and we even have our own elementary school.

I think most of the residents of Roswell are pleased to have a large Air Force base so close because of the jobs and income the base provides, but they have their own small town also, and the Air Force people keep moving in and out all the time. I will be happy to return to Walker and Roswell, even though the weather will be hot all day, cool at night, and the sand never stops blowing.

Panetta and I keep busy with our work. Winds change after a few hours, and a cloud deck gradually builds below. We adjust our headings as we go.

On my return from the dome, I ask Radio, as I do every so often, "Any news from the flight deck?"

Sergeant Snell removes his headset and tells me, "Engine number four is down. Scanner called in smoke on number four, and the flight deck got a engine four fire light for a few seconds, but it's out now. I doubt if they will try to start up number four again on this flight. Kind of early to lose an engine. We still have a long way to go."

I tell him "Thank you" and nod my understanding at what he is telling me. The news that we are losing an engine so early makes me feel a little unsettled myself.

We can see Wake Island through broken clouds as it passes four miles to our south. Shallow turquoise water forms a necklace around the atoll, and small waves break on the sandy beaches. From our altitude, I cannot see any green growth at all. The beaches are just a few feet above the ocean, with blue-green water beyond in all directions. I ask Panetta to sit in for me, and I fall asleep atop flight bags on the radio room floor.

I wake up and check the time. I find that I have been sleeping for a little over half an hour. I sit up, and all looks normal and routine.

Panetta looks back at me, smiles, and I slowly stand up and walk forward.

"Everything okay?" I ask.

"Winds are steady and we still have broken clouds below. I gave the flight deck one small change in heading about ten minutes ago. Water, water."

"It will be a long night."

I turn on the LORAN set, even though we are too far south to expect to receive a signal. Panetta moves into the radio room. The LORAN has a green signal line, but it is intermittent and moves across the screen constantly. As I expected, we are too far south and the signal beacon towers don't reach this far. I will try again later on. We are going to lose celestial in an hour or so. I climb up to the dome, shoot, and plot another fix. The sun is getting low in the sky.

A half-hour later, I shoot one more set of sun readings. The fix plots well, and a little later, I am treated to a sky of spectacular colors as the light of the setting sun behind us reflects off the low band of clouds.

Now comes the time of day that is most frustrating. Sun is too low for a fix, and the sky not dark enough to see the stars. I dead-reckon, knowing each plot is less accurate than the previous one. I'm forced to assume an unchanging wind speed and direction because I have no better information. The LORAN set gives no help, although I continue to adjust the input hoping to find a signal I can use. I drink a whole bottle of water and time moves slowly. LORAN still no help. I climb up to the celestial dome even though I know it's too early, and I look anyway. Panetta is sleeping and I sit. I would rather be sleeping than waiting. I set my head on my arms on the desk. The sky darkens a bit, and I check the dome again. I can see in the east that the sky is a little darker. I try the LORAN one more time out of frustration, but there are no usable signals.

I need three stars. One star will plot as a line on my chart. We will be located somewhere on that line. Two target stars will provide two lines that cross. I would settle for that right now, because where they cross would be a reasonable estimate of position. Three-star observation would give me three lines forming a small triangle, and our location would be at the center of the triangle. The smaller the triangle, the more accurate the observation.

Panetta comes forward, bleary eyed. He looks out the greenhouse and says, "Shit, are we still blind? No sunglasses? No sun? No stars?"

"We need to dead-reckon for a little longer now. It will be dark enough soon," I say.

Panetta is just as frustrated as I am, and there isn't a damn thing we can do about it but wait it out.

"I'm going up to take a look anyway," Panetta says.

He climbs up to the celestial dome. I guess he figures it's better doing nothing while looking out the dome as it is doing nothing while staring across the radar room.

He comes back down. "Arcturus is the only target I can find, and it's barely showing, but I took a sighting on it any way.

"I'll get out of the way," I said. "You plot."

I have a piece of fried chicken and then try to clean my greasy fingers. I look over Panetta's shoulder.

He says, "Arcturus plots okay."

He crosses the star line with our dead-reckoning track.

"So now we know that we are somewhere over the Pacific, west of Hawaii. Make you feel better?" I ask.

He looks at me and manages a smile.

That calls for some more chicken. I sit in the radio room.

"Sergeant Snell," I yell, "what do you hear from upstairs?"

"Number six is down. Temperature too high, too long. That's number four and number six, both on the same side, and we are still short of Hawaii."

That sure as hell isn't good news. I cannot think of a positive response, so I keep quiet.

Panetta calls out, "I'm going up to take another look."

I return to the navigator's position and look out the greenhouse. Two engines out on the same side this early in the flight. Not good at all. Panetta is up at the dome for quite a while. I sure hope that he finds three target stars showing. He comes down the steps with a big smile on his face.

"Got three," he says.

I move out of the way so he can have the satisfaction of plotting.

"Hundred fifteen miles south of course and a half hour out of Hawaii," he says, then grins.

I smile back and give him a high-five. No need telling him about having two engines off line so early in the flight.

"Call in a correction to take us over Honolulu rather than bypass," I tell him. "I'd feel a hell of a lot better if we could see some land and lights."

Paul calls the flight deck with a new heading and ETA for Honolulu, and I go sit in the radio room. After a while, by looking forward from the radio room through the greenhouse, I can see the glow of lights from Honolulu in the distance. I enjoy just watching the glow grow stronger. The clouds below are still broken, but now with 75-percent coverage. In the darkening sky, Honolulu looks good. I climb up to the dome and take a three-star observation and plot. A decent fix. After a while, I call the flight deck.

"A new heading for San Diego," I tell them, "zero seven zero degrees."

"Pilot to Navigator, understand zero seven zero degrees to San Diego."

This is the long leg to the coast. The coastline will be a welcome sight. We will probably have a wind shift as we approach the coastline, and some significant weather at our altitude. We still have 75-percent cloud cover below. There is just the black Pacific to see down there anyway. Scattered thin clouds above, so celestial is still easy. Drone from the engines is loud and steady. *I could sure use a hot shower, a very long, very hot shower.* I feel hot and sweaty, and I smell bad. *California, we're on our way.*

* * * * *

The first time I saw California was at the beginning of summer between my second and third year at college. I was studying Architecture at Rensselaer Polytechnic Institute located in upstate New York in the city of Troy. In the summer between semesters, the campus closed down and I had to move out of the dormitories. During the first summer between semesters, I had rented a room near campus and found a job in a restaurant. Since I had worked in a restaurant while in high school, that worked out real well. Second summer, I moved into the same rented room, but couldn't find a job of any kind. The economy was down and lots of people were looking for work.

My family had moved to California three years earlier, but they were having a tough time themselves. I had seventy dollars left and decided that I would hitchhike to California. At that time, hitchhiking was a reasonable way to travel and not as dangerous as it is today. I left most of my clothes and everything else I owned, which wasn't much, at my landlord's house and packed my gym bag.

Next morning, I took a city bus west to the end of the line, then stuck out my thumb for a ride. I slept in YMCA's almost every night. It was interesting to find out that almost every small town that I traveled through had a YMCA. The Young Men's Christian Association usually had a small building where young men from town could gather and usually had a few simple bedrooms to rent out for a night to young male travelers. I ate only when I absolutely had to. Over the span of about a week, I was able to get rides all the way from Troy, New York, to the eastern edge of our western desert. I looked at the desert and pictured myself, some night, stranded at a crossroad in the open desert with no choice but to sleep on the ground with the snakes.

I found a bus station in the town I was in at the time, put all the money I had left on the counter of the ticket window, and asked the gal at the window for a ticket as far west as my money would take me. The ticket I bought was to downtown Santa Monica in California, and she even gave me two dollars change. On the bus, I slept most of the way and ate popcorn washed down with water. When I arrived at a bus terminal in Santa Monica, I walked the few blocks from the bus terminal to see the Pacific Ocean for the first time. Unforgettable beach and ocean; it was like a picture postcard. All the people were suntanned and they smiled at me.

I then hitchhiked from Santa Monica to a small town called Calabasas, where my family lived. I had not told them that I was hitchhiking, so they all thought I was still in Troy in upstate New York. They were shocked, surprised and happy to see me. I walked in their front door and it was a good homecoming. They were all living in this tiny rental house and were struggling to make ends meet, but it was good to be home. That was the first time I had been to California. Calabasas was surrounded by orange trees and pig farms.

After a few days, I found a job digging trenches for water lines on a ranch close to home. I was home with family, and it was the best summer that I could remember. Summer didn't last long enough.

In September, the money that I had earned wasn't enough, so the family helped me with money to buy a bus ticket back to Troy and school. I promised myself that someday I would live in California. I haven't made it yet, but have I gotten as far west as Roswell, New Mexico.

* * * * *

I am grateful to be able to find the stars I need through the 25-percent cloud cover above. The star shots show our location only twenty miles south of course and paralleling our planned route, so we hold our heading. Through the long night, Panetta and I take turns navigating and sleeping. Radar is happy to occasionally get a return from a ship below rather than just screen static. He sleeps at his station with little trouble and wakes up once in a while to check his systems.

The sun is not above the horizon yet, but the sky is less dark in the east directly off our nose.

I search the LORAN system. Closest transmitting tower on the West Coast of North America is the Middleton Site. It is also the most southerly transmitter. We are unable to receive Middleton, but I keep trying during our blind time between the sun and the stars. Makes me feel as if I'm doing something useful, but it is frustrating and really not useful at all.

Panetta is at the celestial dome, looking at stars that are fading fast as the sky grows lighter.

"Two stars available," he says, "and that's the last for tonight."

I plot the crossed lines and we maintain our heading. Navigating by dead reckoning is all that we have for a while now until the sun is high enough. If we continue to fly east, we are bound to find ourselves somewhere on the West Coast. Not as hard as looking for Guam, a five-mile by eight-mile island in the South Pacific. If we make landfall "somewhere on the coast," though, it is not going to make Kingby very happy. We will have to do a little better than that.

I waste more of my time and energy at the LORAN receiver, and Paul is already up at the dome waiting for the sun. Time passes at a damn slow pace, and I turn off the useless LORAN.

Panetta clumps down the stairs. "First sun reading," he says.

We find that we are still south of course and drifting farther south.

"Navigator to Pilot."

"Pilot here."

"Navigator. New heading zero six five degrees San Diego."

"Acknowledge new heading San Diego zero six five degrees."

"Paul," I say, "when we complete the turn and settle down, I'll use the dome to confirm our position and then another fix in thirty minutes will give us a decent track to work with."

He nods, sits, and leans back against the bulkhead. Ten minutes later, I finish at the dome and I again quiz Sergeant Snell on the way down about the status of our B-36.

"About the same. Engines four and six not turning. Everything else looks steady."

I plot the fix. The sun is now bright and climbing. I put my arms on the chart table and my head on my arms. When I lift my head, Panetta has already taken a sighting on the sun. I move out of the way and he plots, and the track looks good. We will pass San Diego ten miles north of planned course. We are feet-dry over the beautiful Southern California coastline, and Panetta is sitting at the greenhouse enjoying the view while map-reading. I look over at Radar. His scope is active and he has been tracking our path for quite a while. Everyone is feeling better.

Chapter Fourteen

Walker Air Force Base

I walk back to the radio compartment and ask Sergeant Snell, "Anything new I should know about?"

His brow is furrowed, and his eyes look a little too tired. "Engines number four and six are still offline, and temperature on number one is too high but still turning. The engineer is watching number one and doesn't like what he sees. Major Kingby is talking to Luke Air Force Base outside of Phoenix," Snell says.

Doesn't sound good to me. I nod a thank-you. This is becoming a worrisome flight. We continue to check our position with map-reading and celestial shots of the sun. The Colorado River is below us, and we are able to confirm our position.

"Navigator to Pilot."

"Pilot."

"New heading to Phoenix zero eight five degrees."

"Pilot to Navigator, confirm heading zero eight five degrees. I need your estimated time to Phoenix and time direct to Walker."

I quickly work out the times. Something is happening and it's not good. *Get it right.*

"Navigator to Pilot."

"Pilot, go ahead."

"Time in route to Phoenix, one hour seven minutes. Time in route direct to Walker, three hours five minutes."

"Pilot, understand one hour seven minutes Phoenix; three hours five minutes Walker."

"Navigator confirms."

Silence. Only the engines throbbing.

"Panetta," I say, "map-reading is slim. I see high desert and nothing much else. Let's go to celestial every twenty minutes, and I will continue to try to map-read."

Panetta is on the move. When he completes his sighting, I plot the fix and ask him to check my work.

"Looks good to me."

"Okay. Looks good to me, too. Let's take another sighting in twenty minutes."

After a while, Panetta says, "Shall I take another look at the sun? It's been about twenty minutes."

I nod okay. When he returns, I plot the fix and call for a small change in heading to take us directly over Phoenix. Cloud cover below us still at 75 percent. Over Phoenix, I call the flight deck and give them a new heading of zero nine five degrees to Walker.

"Pilot to Navigator. Confirm zero nine five degrees to Walker."

The pilot completes the turn.

"Pilot to crew. Everybody get a headset on. Thirty seconds."

Thirty seconds later: "Major Kingby to crew. We are over Phoenix, have just completed our turn and are one and one-half hours out of Walker Air Force Base. Engines number four and six have been shut down, and we are watching number one, which is turning but reading high temperature. All jets are powered up and in idle. I have been in contact with the tower at Luke near Phoenix and have made them aware of our situation. If we have to shut down number one, I will declare an in-flight emergency and at that time I will decide whether to continue on to Walker or return to Luke. The flight deck will immediately make you aware of any changes. Navigator, compute a point of no return. Major Kingby out."

Four minutes later: "Navigator to Pilot."

"Pilot."

"I read present time at 1206. Estimate Walker at 1352 hours. Point of no return at 1259 hours."

Flight Deck to Navigator: "Point of no return at 1259."

I check cloud cover through the greenhouse, and estimate fifty percent cloud cover below.

"Panetta," I call, "we are over the Rockies and cloud cover above is now increasing. Take a look out the dome."

Panetta returns. "Cloud cover above almost 100 percent. No sun available."

We both concentrate on map-reading. Pilot needs to know where we are at any time. We are flying over mountains about six or seven thousand feet high. The Continental Divide. Few features or landmarks to guide us. I dead-reckon.

"Navigator to Pilot."

"Pilot here."

"Time is 1254. Five minutes to point of no return," I tell the pilot.

"Pilot, understand five minutes."

Silence on the intercom. Ten minutes pass. Phoenix is gone, and we are committed to Walker. Then another ten minutes drags on. Panetta taps me on the shoulder and points forward through the greenhouse.

"Looks like Route 85, running north-south with River Rio Grande paralleling on the east side!" Panetta says.

"Right on," I respond.

"Navigator to Pilot."

"Pilot."

"Revise ETA. Walker at 1348 hours."

An excited voice on the intercom: "Flight Deck, left-side scanner. Black smoke coming out of engine number one."

"Pilot, understand smoke at number one. Light or moderate?"

Scanner responds, "Started light, now heavy. A flame just shot out of the back of engine number one!"

"Crew, this is Second Pilot. Major Kingby is at the controls. We are shutting down engine number one. Fire suppression system activated. All jets powered up. Prepare to take positions for an emergency landing on my call."

I scan out the greenhouse. Everyone is waiting. Waiting. We keep descending ... and waiting.

"Crew, take positions for emergency landing, now," is the call from the second pilot.

Major Heller shuts down his entire radar system and at the same time climbs out of his seat.

"Panetta," I yell, "radio room!"

I loosen my seat belt and turn to the rear. The plane is rocking left and right from ground turbulence, but it looks as if it is still holding altitude. Heller has his chute in hand and is almost into the radio compartment. He turns and looks back. I look in his eyes and see no fear. I see resignation. Calm resignation.

I have no control. My eyes feel wide open with fear bleeding through. My throat is squeezed shut and I need water. *I have no control.*

Panetta moves past me, his eyes turned toward the floor. He is looking for his chute pack. We need our chute packs to use as padding while we sit on the floor. He scoops up his chute and keeps moving. My chute is on the floor touching my left leg. I pick it up and follow Panetta. I can hear and feel the engines surging and the whine of the jets. Feels as if we are losing altitude, but still controlled.

We are all jammed together, side by side, with our backs against the forward bulkhead. I have my knees drawn up with the chute tight between my chin and my knees. Radio has his back against the bulkhead, has his headset on with a long wire cord from his station so that he can still monitor the intercom. We all look around, not at each other, but mostly at the floor. We cannot see outside.

Radio bellows, "Engineer is dumping fuel. Tower clears us for a straight-in approach. No pattern. Yellow trucks on the way."

I close my eyes and listen. We're descending. The sound of the engines is decreasing, the jets are whining, and I can feel the plane rocking left, right, left, right. Noise from the engines rises and falls as the pilots work the controls. *So this is how it is. Can't see the ground or the sky. I have no control.*

When I was about ten years old, we lived in Brooklyn, New York. I and my brother Joe, who was one year older, would take the subway to Coney Island on Saturdays right after breakfast. We would go to the beach and then eat at Nathan's Hot Dogs, but mainly we went to go to Steeplechase Park. We always went on the roller-coaster ride because Joe would call me a wimp if I didn't go on. I would hold on tight to the bar in front of me, terrified as the car climbed up the sloping track. Clank, clank, clank as a chain pulled us up to the top.

Couldn't see the ground. I remember that I was scared because I had no control. Sick stomach.

I feel like I am back at Coney Island again. No control.

I guess the Air Force studied the problem and decided the best place for us to ride out a landing is where we are, in the radio compartment. Wish I had something to hold onto besides my chute. Probably makes little difference.

Engines sound as if they are being pulled back, and we keep descending slowly. The ground turbulence feels more severe. Nose of our B-36 is now bobbing up and down, and we are still fighting the ground turbulence. Vibrations are getting stronger. Must be a bitch trying to land this monster with three engines out. Guess we should be grateful that all three are not on the same side. If they were all on the same side, I don't think we would have stayed aloft this long.

I look around again. *Kingby will bring it in.* Everyone is braced and rigid, fighting his own terror within. I'm in a sweat and trying to breath slowly. Waiting.

"Two minutes," Snell calls out.

He takes off his headset and covers his ears with his hands, looking down.

Engines are louder, jets whining. Nose pulls up! *Two minutes, hell!* My chest is tight. I open my eyes and then squeeze them shut.

We rock left. I can feel the left main gear hit the runway. Tires squeal, and we bounce up and off. The left gear slams down again, hits hard, and stays down. Plane rocks to the right and, slam, the right gear hits the runway and stays down. We're rolling too fast.

BOOM!

What's that?

I push my back harder against the bulkhead. The nose is still up and we're going too fast! The nose gear slams down. BOOM! BOOM! Tires must be blowing! I'm being pushed harder against the bulkhead. Brakes? Nose jerking right, then left. Slowing down. Left side dragging. Slow lean to the left. We're moving too fast! Engine noise drops off and then ...

Loud!

Loud!

Engines in reverse? Left side is going down! Metal scraping on the left side. Horrible scraping noise, louder and louder, on the left side.

153

"We're crashing!" I yell.

I'm yelling in my head, but no sound comes out. Bright flashes through my closed eyes. Sliding left. Tremendous noises. Tearing metal. We're coming apart! Sunlight and darkness. Sliding. I slam into the left sidewall of the compartment. *Tipping over!* Everybody is sliding on top of me. I yell.

Light, then darkness. I don't hurt.

I'm okay.

* * * * *

I hear voices, talking softly. Can't hear what they are saying. I really don't care what they are saying. Voices fade. Voices again. *I'm not dead.*

I hurt like something hit me on the side of my head. I open my eyes. I'm in bed, but I feel light, like I'm floating. My eyes are blurred and they feel wet. They must have given me something to make me feel okay.

No voices now. I'm looking at a light on a white ceiling, and I hurt all over now. I can feel my arms and legs, and they hurt like the rest of me. Feels as if I have a tube or something up my nose. *Have to get rid of that.* I'm not dead, but I'm pretty well beat up. Someone is on my left, and I try to turn my head to look that way, but my head is held in place. *Can't move my head!* I start to panic. I roll my eyes left.

Betty is standing close. Bright eyes, sun on her hair, and dressed in a very white nurse's uniform.

She smiles and says, "Hi, hon."

I say, "Hi," but it sounds like "Haaaaa."

I feel her hand on top of mine. The room is cool, but her hand is soft and warm.

"Everybody else?" I manage.

Betty hesitates. "Lieutenant Perez received a head injury and died instantly."

Silence.

"Everyone else is hurt and recovering." Betty's voice is soft, but I can hear her. "Your right leg is broken above the knee, and your right arm is broken near your shoulder. You look terrible right now, but the doctor says you will be fine. Major Kingby has head injuries and a broken left shoulder. Others have broken bones, and you all look like you've been in a bad fight and lost. Everyone is going to be okay."

I can see other people in the room now. Everyone is smiling. I try to smile, but can't tell if I succeed or not.

AUTHOR AT NAVIGATOR STATION

Epilogue

Crash Landing at Walker AFB

The left landing gear touched down hard, bounced once, and then stayed down. The right landing gear hit the runway very hard, but stayed down. Left gear tires blew. Nose wheel came down hard, and the nose landing gear collapsed.

The left-side jets hit the runway and both sheared off. The fuselage separated at the leading edge of the wing and bomb bay number one.

With the nose gear still intact, the forward section fell on its left side and slid forward, rotating around the nose gear.

The right gear collapsed, and the aft section scraped and slid on its belly. No fire.

Gunners in the aft section had secured all the mattresses against the front bulkhead of the compartment and sat with their backs against the mattresses. Rescue teams evacuated all men in the rear compartment through side ports, all with broken bones, some with concussions.

Flight deck crew had heavy injuries and were evacuated through pilots' windows and Plexiglas dome over the pilots' positions.

Crew members in radio room were all wedged into front left side of radio room. All had broken bones and some received concussions.

All injured crew members recovered and returned to flight status. Major Kingby, the most severely injured survivor, had a good recovery and was assigned to a position at Wing staff.

Crew List

Aircraft Commander: Major Kingby
Second Pilot: Captain Harris
Third Pilot: First Lieutenant Perez
First Engineer: Captain Cruz
Second Engineer: None assigned
Radar: Major Heller, Bob
Navigator: First Lieutenant Hall, William
Observer: Second Lieutenant Panetta, Paul
First Radio: Master Sergeant Snell, Lou
Second Radio: None assigned
Chief Gunner/Scanner: Technical Sergeant Gordon

Author's
Historical Note

In 1948, the Cold War between the US and the USSR was already raging. The Berlin Airlift was followed by the Soviets' testing of their first atomic bomb in 1949. This caused the United States military to seek a system capable of delivering large, heavy first-generation nuclear bombs on selected military targets in the USSR.

At the time, the B-36 aircraft was the only military system the United States possessed capable of filling this need, and it became the primary system for delivery of nuclear weapons. The Army and Navy were both working on the problem, but in 1948 did not have the capability to deliver a weapon. The crews manning this aircraft knew that they and their B-36 bombers were playing an important role in the defense of the United States in the Cold War. All B-36 bombers were assigned to the Strategic Air Command, and that component of the United States Air Force became our primary Cold War "shield."

The B-36 bomber was modified and improved so that it was capable of flying at high altitudes, out of reach of all piston fighter planes and all jet interceptors. The original design of the B-36 could not carry atomic or hydrogen weapons. Later models were modified so as to make the B-36 capable of delivering these weapons. Later, in order to carry the MK-17 hydrogen bomb, two bomb bays of the aircraft had to be modified into one—to contain the huge bulk and length of the weapon.

The B-36 never did drop a bomb on enemy territory. The plane fulfilled its mission, though, as a deterrent during the Cold War years against the USSR.

In 1954, production of the B-36 was ended, as its replacement, the B-52, was being delivered to the frontline air crews. The last planes built were the B-36J configuration, known as the Featherweight Model. The Featherweight Model was the Air Force's final attempt to keep the B-36 operational until enough B-52's were on the line to fully replace the old B-36's.

The B-36J Featherweight had all defensive gunnery, extend and retract mechanisms, and fire control systems removed, except for the tail gun. It was stripped of all nonessential equipment and crew comforts. Crew was reduced from fifteen to nine. All possible modifications were made to reduce weight. One of the bomb bays was modified to carry 2,700 additional gallons of fuel.

The B-36J flew at a 50,000-foot altitude, 10,000 feet higher than any interceptor aircraft, with a combat range of 4,500 nautical miles and a combat speed of 423 miles an hour.

When interceptor aircraft and missiles were developed to reach the B-36J at 50,000 feet, a last resort tactic was developed, called the "flip delivery." The J model aircraft, on a combat mission, would fly at normal altitudes, but when about to enter enemy-controlled territory, the aircraft would drop down so as to approach its target at 200 feet above terrain in order to escape radar detection. Near the target, the B-36 would nose up, climbing as fast as possible, and when almost vertical at as high an altitude as possible, it would execute the flip delivery. The plane would release the weapon, and the aircraft and the bomb would continue vertical flight until the bomb would loop out and over and descend on the target. As soon as the weapon separated, the B-36J would immediately turn away from its target and run at top speed to avoid the effects of the blast.

Aircraft damage from the nuclear blast? Exposure of the crew to radiation? The Air Force ran many tests, but no one really knew what the effect would be on the aircraft or the crew. The crews who flew the Featherweight knew that the odds of them flying another day were not too good.

The B-36 was never fun to fly for the pilots or the crew. Twenty-two-hour training flights were common, with the entire crew in full flight gear for most of the time in the air. This included a floatation device when over water, an oxygen mask, and arctic gear at extreme altitudes. Most of the crew, when they had the opportunity, slept in their seats at their flight stations or on the floor close by.

Made in the USA
Lexington, KY
08 March 2017